ORIGIN OF MAGIC

DRAGON'S GIFT THE PROTECTOR BOOK 3

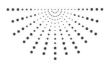

LINSEY HALL

To Tori, who is fantastic.

CHAPTER ONE

The streets of Magic's Bend were eerily quiet as I turned toward Darklane, the part of town where the black magic practitioners lived. Rain splattered on the windshield of Fabio, my Dodge Challenger Hellcat and the one true love of my life.

At least, that's what I told him when I turned him on.

"Where is everyone?" Del peered out of the passenger window at the empty sidewalks and ramshackle Victorian buildings that lined the main street in Darklane.

"No idea." It was normally a bit quieter on this side of town, but tonight it was like a cemetery. It was nearly eight. People should be headed to dinner and bars. "It's almost as if everyone got a memo that said, get out of dodge."

Del laughed. "Like the cops are gonna show."

Police didn't come near Darklane much, but if they were coming, the people that lived here would probably scram. Darklaners weren't all bad—just as all dark magic wasn't bad—but a lot of them were.

Just being here made my hair stand on end. But we needed information, and this was the place to get it.

"There it is." Del pointed toward the Apothecary's Jungle, a three-story building with ornate trim. Black grime obscured the purple paint.

"There's nowhere to park." Cars lined the street in front of the shop owned by our friends, Blood Sorceresses Mordaca and Aerdeca.

"It's after business hours. Why are there so many people here?"

"No idea." I passed the house, finally finding a spot about thirty meters down. At least the rain had let up and was now a mere drizzle.

I cut the engine and turned, grabbing the box off the back seat. I climbed out of Fabio and joined Del on the sidewalk. She zipped up her black leather jacket to keep the drizzle out, but the rain glittered on her dark hair.

Her blue eyes went to the box I carried, which was small and locked with a padlock. A leather strap, almost like one on a messenger bag, hung off the side. I looped it crosswise over my back, securing it so that a thief couldn't grab the box and run. I wasn't taking any chances.

He'd have to stop and fight me, and there was no chance I'd let him win. The box contained a rare artifact—a clay vase that was thousands of years old and enchanted with an unfamiliar magic. It was technically called a beaker, even though it didn't look like one of the glass vials favored by scientists, and we needed to know more about the strange magic it possessed. This beaker was our only clue to finding a dangerous mob boss who was threatening the city.

Hence, Darklane on a Thursday night.

"Got it?" Del nodded to the box.

"Yep." I clutched it to my chest and started walking.

It'd been four days since we'd stolen this beaker back from the dangerous criminal who'd originally taken it from us. I'd been injured in the fight and was just recently back on my feet.

Now, we were on the hunt for answers. It was our only clue and our only hope of finding the bastard.

As we neared the Apothecary's Jungle, the sound of music floated down the street.

"It's coming from their place," Del said.

"Yeah." It was some kind of swanky party music. I glanced at Del. "Are they having a party?"

"Could be. They live above the shop."

We neared the Apothecary's Jungle, the music growing louder, and climbed the stairs to the front door, which was slightly cracked open. Del and I looked at each other, then shrugged and pushed the door open.

It *was* a party.

"So this is where everyone went," Del said.

There were so many people jammed into the space that it had to be most of the folks in Darklane.

Though I'd known Aerdeca and Mordaca must have social lives, we weren't good enough friends to know exactly what they did on their down time. Apparently they liked to throw rocking parties for every variety of supernatural in Darklane. Weres, fae, demons, and mages were all dressed in their best, sipping fancy cocktails in every color of the rainbow.

Their magical signatures clashed on the air—scents, sounds, feelings, and tastes all representing a variety of types of magic. Some of these folks were strong and dangerous. The rotten scent of dark magic hovered at the edges. Though it wasn't the predominant signature, some of these folks were trouble. I gathered my magic close, ready to conjure a weapon.

Half a dozen people turned to look at us, their lips turning down.

"Tough crowd," Del muttered.

"No kidding." It was almost as if they could smell that we were regular, law-abiding citizens. Ignoring the fact that we possessed forbidden FireSoul magic, because they couldn't possibly know that. We kept that magic locked up tight, unnoticeable to anyone but us. "Might as well act like we belong."

I pushed my way through the crowd, shivering at the feel of the dark magic brushing up against me. Del stuck by my side. Power in numbers, that was our motto. We passed through the small foyer to a larger room on the left.

In the corner, I spotted Mathias, the big were-lion that Mordaca dated. But she wasn't at his side.

A man bumped into my side. Instinctively, I clutched the box to my chest. I didn't know what exactly the spell on this thing did, but I knew it was important and I sure as heck wasn't going to lose it.

"Careful," I muttered.

The man turned, his brows raised. He was handsome, in a sleek way. Tall, with blond hair and glittering blue eyes. Rich playboy. Wall Street, if Magic's Bend had a Wall Street, with a cunning light in his eyes that made me shiver.

And *fangs.*

A vampire.

"Excuse me." His gaze traveled up and down my body, then drifted to Del. Appreciation lit his eyes. "Ladies. Don't you both look lovely tonight?"

I glanced down at my T-shirt. A wiener dog wearing a hotdog bun popped up above the box. I loved a bad pun, but most people didn't find that particularly charming. Annoying, was more like it. I looked up at the vampire. "Really?"

"I like different." His gaze traveled between us.

I looked at Del. "I guess that's us."

"Yep."

He grinned, charming in a scary way. "Indeed it is."

"Well, we're not here for that." I already had one hot vampire to deal with—Ares, one of the three members of the Vampire Court. He put this guy to shame. "But you have a good evening."

He grinned, his fangs flashing in the light, and inclined his head. "Enjoy your night. But if you change your mind…"

"We're good."

He smiled and nodded goodbye. At least he was gracious.

We hurried off through the crowd, dodging fae wings and shifter tails. Apparently some people were having such a good time they let their inner animal out a bit.

Near the back of the long living room, a crowd of people faced the wall. Between the figures, I caught a glimpse of a tall black bouffant, then a flash of red lipstick. Mordaca. We slipped through the crowd, finding our two friends holding court in large wingback chairs.

Mordaca, with her massive midnight bouffant and scarlet lipstick, looked like the cousin of Elvira, Mistress of the Dark. She wore so much black eye makeup that it looked like a mask, and her glittering red dress plunged low between her breasts. I'd never seen her out of her trademark black, but this definitely worked on her. Claw-like nails were painted a gleaming black that shined in the light as she held out a hand to be kissed.

At her side sat Aerdeca, wearing a striking silver gown that flowed like water over her slender form. The cloth appeared to be made of pure metal. Liquid silver. Though she looked like Mordaca's good sister, with her blond hair and lightly made-up face, she was just as deadly and twice as dark.

Appearances could be deceiving.

Except for this situation, where it appeared that people were coming to pay their respects to royalty.

"These chicks are weird," Del muttered.

"But they've always had our back."

"Ain't that the truth?" Del grinned. "Gotta love 'em."

I wiggled my way between a couple of shifters—foxes, from the look of their golden eyes—and ignored their growls of displeasure.

Aerdeca glanced up, her blue gaze meeting mine. Surprise flashed in her eyes and her golden brows rose. "Nix. Del."

"Hey, Aerdeca, you got a second?" I said.

She glanced at Mordaca, who pulled her hand away from a slavering fae and grinned at us, her red lips glinting in the light.

"We do." Aerdeca waved her hand at the people standing around me, the dismissal clear.

They scattered.

"Handy trick," I said.

"Isn't it though?" Mordaca's voice was raspy and deep, a direct contrast to Aerdeca's lilting tones.

"I guess our invitation got lost in the mail." It actually kinda stung—I really *had* thought we were friends.

"We sent one. By strippergram." Aerdeca grinned. "No one was home."

"Strippergram?"

Aerdeca made a little hand motion, a twirl of her finger. "You know, dancing policeman, takes his trousers off and the invitation is tied to—"

Del laughed and I thrust out my hand, palm forward. "We get it. We get it."

"Not a problem, though," Mordaca said. "I think that was when you were busy being accused of murder. We understand why you couldn't get back to us."

I grimaced. "Thoughtful."

"Always." Aerdeca smiled.

"How'd you know about the accusation, though?" Del asked.

"We know a lot of people. They know a lot of things." Aerdeca gestured to the crowd that now lingered in circles, sipping cocktails and chatting. Despite the formality of the hand-kissing that the sisters seemed to insist upon, everyone looked like they were having a good time.

"I didn't know you were getting into the information business." As far as I knew, they'd primarily stuck to selling blood spells and potions from their shop. Now they were establishing themselves in a serious position of power.

"It was time to expand the empire," Mordaca said.

Well, if anyone could do it, it was them. Though what their empire would do, exactly...

Probably better if I didn't stick my nose in it. Darklane business was not my business, especially if I liked my head right where it was. On my shoulders.

"What do you need?" Aerdeca nodded at the box in my hands. "I assume it has to do with that box?"

"Yeah." I clutched it closer to my chest. "We were hoping you could take a look at it."

"It'll cost you." Aerdeca rubbed her fingers together.

"No problem." There were no friendly discounts with Mordaca and Aerdeca.

They nodded and stood, starting toward the crowd. People parted like the red sea. We followed them into the workshop at the back. Aerdeca ran her fingertip around the doorframe, igniting a flare of magic.

Protection charm, now disabled.

She entered and flipped on the light. The long table in the middle of the room held only a spray of dried flowers, but the shelves against the wall were packed with jars and bottles and boxes. I didn't know the full extent of what they did back here, just that their magic involved blood and treaded the line between light and dark. Hence their names, Blood Sorceresses. They'd helped us a number of times in the past, and hopefully they'd come through this time too.

Aerdeca and Mordaca walked toward the table, then took up a space behind it, as if it were their desk.

"Let's see what's in that box." Mordaca eyed it.

"I hope it's not a head," Aerdeca said.

"I hope it is one." Mordaca sounded a hell of a lot like Wednesday Addams.

"No head." I slipped the strap over my shoulders and put the box on the table. It took a second to fish the key out of my pocket, but by the time I'd popped open the lock and pried the lid off the box, Aerdeca and Mordaca were leaning forward, interest gleaming in their eyes.

"Dang." Disappointment shadowed Mordaca's voice.

"Not at all." Interest lit Aerdeca's eyes. "Anything that ugly has to have some serious magic in it."

"It's not ugly." Ire warmed my belly. Sure, the vase was made of rough clay, with simple incised decoration, but it wasn't *ugly*. And it was thousands of years old, crafted by an ancient culture that had lived in Northern England before the advent of writing. "It's special. Very special. But how do you know it has serious magic?"

"Why else would you be interested in it? You can't display it on your mantle. Not looking like that." Aerdeca gestured with white-tipped fingernails.

"I couldn't display it because it's illegal to take artifacts," I said. Except that this one couldn't remain in its tomb—not with the mob boss after it. "But that's not the point. The point is that we want to know what kind of magic it contains."

A self-satisfied smile curved Aerdeca's lips.

"Yeah, yeah. You were right." I grinned at her. "It has serious magic. Now tell us what you know. We're desperate."

"Who else have you asked for help?" Mordaca asked.

"Everyone." Which was why we were here. I didn't like blood magic, but this was the end of our line. We'd spent the day hunting answers but come up short. Normally, our friend Dr. Garriso at the Museum for Magical History was able to help us with things like this. But he'd come up empty, too.

"No one could give us a clue," Del said.

"We were hoping you could do a spell to see what kind of magic it once contained."

Aerdeca nodded. "We can try, at least."

Mordaca reached out and hovered her hand over the beaker, her face intense. Aerdeca joined her. They looked like they were trying to feel for a signature. Eventually, Mordaca touched the beaker with her fingertip.

She gasped. "Evil."

Aerdeca touched her white-tipped nail to the clay. Her eyes flared wide. "It was owned by pure evil."

"But the vase itself is not dark," Mordaca said. "Just the stain that the previous owner left upon it."

I glanced at Del. "Do you think that could be the mob boss?"

She nodded. "Likely."

"Is the stain recent?" I asked.

"It is. And the spell that this vase contains… It feels like it has been used recently. The magic—it wavers."

"Do you know what the spell is?" I'd been trying to determine what the enchantment was ever since Cass had brought it back from the tomb in the Yorkshire Dales.

"We can try," Aerdeca said. "But we'll need a donation."

Mordaca raised her wrist to indicate.

I grimaced. "Of course."

"Let me get my tools." Aerdeca turned and bustled around the room, collecting objects while Mordaca retrieved a slender knife from the counter behind her.

Aerdeca returned and laid a shiny slab of black rock on the big table, along with two vials of red and orange potion.

Mordaca raised the knife. "Ready?"

"Yeah." I stuck my wrist out.

Mordaca gestured with the knife. "Hold your wrist over the slab."

I shifted. Mordaca raised the blade and made a thin slice through my flesh at my wrist. Pain flared and I winced as the blood welled to the surface. This was the unfortunate part of blood sorcery. The key ingredient was painful to get to.

I twisted my wrist so that the blood dripped onto the shiny

slab of rock. It pearled on the surface, gleaming dark in the light. Once a small puddle had formed, Aerdeca nodded. "That will be enough."

I withdrew my hand, taking the cloth that Mordaca handed to me. I pressed it against the wound, watching as Aerdeca poured a few drops of the red potion onto the blood, followed by the orange potion.

The mixture sizzled slightly, as if boiling, then Mordaca held her hand over the puddle. I felt her magic flare, the taste of whiskey on the back of my throat.

The liquid flashed with light, then turned to a silvery dust.

"Neat," Del murmured.

"More than neat," Aredeca said. "That's top-level magic."

She picked up the slab of stone and held it near the beaker, then blew the dust onto the clay vase. Magic swirled on the air, feeling like strong ocean breeze against my cheeks. It came from the beaker.

I held my breath as Aerdeca and Mordaca touched the clay surface, closing their eyes for concentration.

"Yes. A terrible person last used this beaker." Aerdeca shuddered.

The mob boss. But what had he wanted with the thing? "What does the enchantment do?"

Mordaca's brow furrowed. "I think... I think it is a revealer of prophecies."

"What?" I asked.

"It's a vessel of truth." Aerdeca's voice was breathless. "There are a few in the world. If you drink from it, you can understand hidden secrets. Information that has been protected or scrambled."

Holy crap. I glanced at Del, who was looking at me with raised brows.

"Can it be used again?" I asked. "Or was it a one-time thing?"

"It could be used again," Aerdeca said.

Excitement flared in my chest.

"How?" Del demanded.

Mordaca frowned. "You must mix a special potion and drink it from the beaker."

"So we need the recipe," I said.

"That's the problem," Aerdeca said. "Whoever made this beaker also knew the recipe for the potion. But this thing is ancient."

"And whoever developed the recipe for the potion has got to be long dead." Something unfamiliar flickered in Mordaca's eyes. Worry, almost. Or fear.

But nah, that was crazy. Mordaca wasn't afraid of anything.

"So there's no one else who could know the recipe?" I asked.

"Only the one who crafted this beaker," Aerdeca said.

Dismay opened a black cavern in my chest. Shit.

"Is there anything else you can tell us?" Del asked.

Mordaca shook her head. "Not about the beaker, no."

Damn.

"Then what do we owe you?" I asked, my mind already racing ahead to how we could turn this devastating information into something good.

Mordaca and Aerdeca spoke at once. "Nothing."

Shocked, my jaw dropped. These women, though friends, would charge you to use their bathroom. "What? Why?"

Aerdeca sighed, her gaze drifting to the beaker. "Whoever used that last… You must stop him, Nix."

I knew that. But how did she? Mordaca and Aerdeca had fought at our side before, but they didn't know about the Triumvirate or our fated tasks.

"We're not stupid," Mordaca said. "You are fighting something stronger than you. Darker than you. This vase makes that clear. The dark magic that is smeared upon it made my skin crawl."

"We won't charge you." Aerdeca's gaze zeroed in on me. "But you must defeat whoever last held this beaker. His evil intentions are all over it. I've never felt darkness like that. And I'm no stranger to black magic."

I shuddered. "I thought you weren't a seer."

"I'm not. But I can read the magic, and that thing scares the shit out of me. Whoever used that beaker last learned something when he drank from the goblet. The vessel of truth untangled a prophecy for him."

Yeah, a prophecy that I wanted to understand. One about dragons that had been encrypted by ancient monks called Cathars. If the mob boss now understood what the prophecy meant, I needed to as well. It was our only link to him. Our only way to find him.

"We know you're meant for something important. We don't know what, but Cass and Del have fought their battles. It is time for yours." Mordaca pointed to the goblet. "This is yours."

My mouth dried. "Yes, it is."

"Well, then, we're not charging you." The corner of Aerdeca's mouth tilted up. "This time."

They had our backs. My back. The message was clear. And terrifying.

Though it was good to have allies, knowing that they—these powerful women—were afraid of whatever was coming made my skin grow cold.

I had to fight something that scared even Aerdeca and Mordaca.

And I had no idea what it was.

CHAPTER TWO

Del and I left the party in silence, climbing into the car. As soon as we were in and had shut the doors, she turned to me. "If we can use our dragon senses to find who made this beaker, I can turn back time so we can speak to him. Get the potion."

"The least we can do is try." Though I had my doubts our dragon senses could work with so little to go on.

I locked the car doors and removed the beaker from the box. The clay was rough under my fingertips, history speaking through the material and the design.

But it wasn't telling me what I needed to know. Who had made this damned thing? And where could I find him? Or his body, since he was probably dead.

I called upon my dragon sense, begging it to help me find the creator. I focused on the feeling of the clay beneath my fingers, the cool irregularity of the surface. But I got nothing. No matter how hard I tried, my dragon sense lay dormant.

Though I'd expected it to be difficult—my dragon sense needed information to work, the more the better—disappointment surged.

I handed the beaker off to Del. "Give it a go."

She took the beaker and closed her eyes. Her magic swelled in the car, bringing with it the scent of fresh soap and the feel of grass beneath my feet. She tried for a full five minutes before opening her eyes. "Nothin'."

"Damn." I pushed the ignition button and pulled away from the curb.

"Looks like this is going to be even tougher than we thought."

"But the mob boss managed. He's already drunk from it or he'd have fought harder for it when we ambushed him. If he succeeded, then we can too." He might be two steps ahead of us every time, but he was proving it was possible.

Del repackaged the beaker in its specially designed box, locking it tight. We drove in silence back to Ancient Magic, where we'd arranged to meet everyone else after a long day of hunting down info. While Del and I had been on beaker duty, the rest were trying to discover the mob boss's whereabouts.

All the way home, the silence was thick as pudding. Worry was the whipped cream on top.

I pulled up to the curb in front of Ancient Magic and cut the engine, then glanced at Del.

Concern glinted in her eyes. "I sure hope someone else found something out."

"No kidding."

I climbed out of the car, grabbing the box and going into the shop. The door was open and Cass was behind the counter, though the shop wasn't officially open for business. After I'd ended up in the hospital a few days ago, we'd shut down the shop to dedicate all our time to hunting the mob boss.

But I already missed this place, with its shelves full of magic and history.

Cass straightened from her slouched position in the chair behind the desk and pushed her red hair back behind her ear. "Any luck?"

"A little." I put the box on the counter. "You?"

14

"Not much. The League of FireSouls knew nothing." Cass had gone to visit the only other FireSouls we knew, an ancient organization that was a bit like a magical Justice League. "But Aidan will be back from the Shifter Council soon."

"Roarke as well," Del said. "Maybe the Order knew something."

Each had gone to see the government that they were loosely affiliated with. Hopefully, the Alpha Council or Order of the Magica would know something useful.

Cass tilted her chin toward the door. "Speak of the devil."

"Devils. Plural," Del said.

I felt him before I saw him, an innate knowing that was new. Ares. Was the connection from the blood he'd given me to heal me after my injuries? Just the idea made me nervous, but it was hard not to make the connection.

Slowly, I turned. Ares walked toward the shop alongside Roarke and Aidan. I hadn't felt their presence like I'd felt his, so this was specific to the vampire.

They stepped through the doorway, single file, each huge and handsome. But I only had eyes for Ares, who looked like a fallen angel.

"Look what I found loitering outside the shop." Aidan hiked a thumb toward Roarke and Ares.

"Hardly loitering," Roarke said. "Good timing, is how I like to think of it."

Ares didn't speak, just looked straight at me, gaze penetrating. It was as if he hadn't seen me in ages, though we'd just parted yesterday. Because of my injuries, and the fact that I'd been asleep for most of three days, we hadn't had much time to talk. I still didn't know where we stood besides being massively attracted to each other. Being around him felt like flame drawn to flame.

Not that it mattered at this precise moment, considering all that we had to deal with. Everyone gathered around the counter. Ares came to stand at my side, close enough that I could smell the cold winter morning scent of his magic and feel the slightest bit of heat from his arm. I shivered.

But he didn't look at me. Which was good. I needed to focus.

"Did anyone learn anything useful?" I asked.

"Strike out with the Order of the Magica," Roarke said. "But I have a couple more contacts I can check tomorrow."

"Aidan?" Cass said. "Any luck with the Alpha Council?"

Aidan, as the Origin and most powerful Shifter, had gone to speak with the governing body of all Shifters.

"A bit," Aidan said. "About fifty years ago, someone similar to our target set up a massive compound about twenty miles from their headquarters at Glencarrough. It was an organized crime operation that recruited young shifters. The Council didn't like it, so they raided the place one night, razing it to the ground."

I nodded, remembering the massive shifter stronghold in the Scottish Highlands. The place was nearly impenetrable. "Could that be our guy? Fifty years is a long time."

The mob boss hadn't looked that old when I'd last seen him. If he was some kind of immortal, we were in big trouble. Immortality was rare, and always a product of strong magic.

"It could be," Aidan said. "They said his power was enormous. But they lost track of him after that night. He abandoned his men."

"Like he did last week." The bastard had flown off in a helicopter, blowing up his compound with a bomb that had nearly killed me. That willingness to abandon all those who worked for him. *With* him. I shuddered.

"Exactly. His men are disposable, his mission is not. But they couldn't say what that mission was." Aidan scrubbed a frustrated hand through his hair.

"Did they say anything else?" I asked.

"Only that his men called him *Drakon.*"

"Dragon?" Fire burned low in my belly. "He doesn't deserve that name."

"No. But it's what he's after." Ares spoke for the first time, his rough voice and light accent curling around me like a caress at the most inappropriate time.

I turned to him. Despite the exhaustion shadowing his green eyes, he was the handsomest man I'd ever seen.

"Please tell me that the Cathars could help," I said.

While I'd been hunting information about the beaker, Ares had returned to the Cathar stronghold in Southern France where we'd first learned of the prophecy that Drakon sought. Ares shook his head. "They could not help, nor would they. Though they protected the prophecy for centuries, the one who encrypted the prophecy is long dead. They know no more than we do."

Damn. "At least we now have a name. And a few more clues. Maybe we can find someone to read the history of the beaker."

"Tomorrow." Del yawned, the exhaustion of the last two days clearly wearing on her. "For now, let's get some sleep. Start fresh tomorrow."

I couldn't help but feel like we didn't have time to sleep, but my own eyelids were drooping. "Fine. I'm going to keep the beaker in my apartment. It's safest."

It'd go right into my trove, but I didn't want to mention that place to Ares yet. Too private.

"Agreed," Cass said.

I picked up the box containing the beaker and looped the strap over my back, then followed my friends out of the shop, Ares at my side. They stopped to wait for me when I turned to ignite the security charms on the doors.

"Go on ahead." I clutched the box to me and ran my fingertips around the edge of the doorframe.

"See you tomorrow," Del said. A chorus of goodbyes followed, and they headed down the sidewalk toward the door to our apartments.

Ares stood at my side, his presence a constant reminder of the attraction and tension that shimmered under the surface. Every inch of me was so aware of him.

"How are you holding up?" His voice was rougher than normal, no doubt from lack of sleep. He'd been hunting answers as aggressively as the rest of us.

"Fine." I finished igniting the enchantment and turned to him. His shoulders blocked out the light from the streetlamp across the road, bathing him in shadow. "Thanks for helping with this."

"The Vampire Court has a vested interest in this. *I* have a vested interest."

"Because of what Laima said?" A couple days ago, the Vampire goddess of fate had done me a real favor by telling the Vampire Court that they'd better back me up.

"Because I like you, Nix." His green eyes bored into mine. Truth reflected in them.

A smile tugged at the corner of my mouth. "Walk me to my door?"

His lips turned up and he turned. I joined him, walking down the sidewalk toward our apartments. Ares's hand closed around mine, warm and firm. A shiver raced through me. I glanced up, brows raised.

"I shouldn't hold your hand?" he asked, his voice held a hint of playfulness that I'd never heard before. It was so small that I might have imagined it.

"No, I didn't say that." We'd had a rocky start, with the murder accusations and the Vampire Court trials, but this was definitely moving us in a different direction.

I'd had more of his blood after my injuries at Drakon's compound. More than ever, I felt like I got a sense of his feelings. And if I wasn't mistaken, he was totally into me.

I clutched the box to my stomach and held Ares's hand, enjoying the warmth of his touch. We'd only shared a few kisses, but they'd blown my mind. Touching any part of Ares always had the same effect.

I'd seen Cass and Del with their guys and wanted the same thing. Then Ares had shown up—in circumstances that weren't exactly the greatest.

I was still processing, to say the least.

The moon was just a sliver in the sky as we walked, the air chill. Street lamps shed circles of golden light on the sidewalk around us, insulating us in our own little world as we walked.

"I'm headed back to the Vampire Court tonight," Ares said. "I need to pick something up. It's important, or I wouldn't leave. But I can meet you in the morning. We'll start the search fresh."

"Sounds good."

We were only ten feet from the door leading to my apartment when magic crackled on the air. I got a brief whiff of rotten garbage before a hand landed on my shoulder, yanking me backward. I lost my grip on Ares.

Instinctually, I clutched the box to my chest. I conjured a sword as a strong arm wrapped around my waist, heaving me upward. My stomach dropped as panic chilled my skin.

"Nix!" Ares roared. He spun and plowed toward me, his shadow sword already in hand. He thrust the blade near my head. Blood sprayed my cheek, no doubt from the head wound he'd just delivered to my attacker, whose arm loosened around my waist.

From behind Ares, four more figures appeared out of thin air. Demons—huge ones wearing leather vests and carrying big swords.

"Ares! Behind you!" I dove away from the man that Ares had stabbed.

There were seven total, demons of all shapes and sizes. All were different. Horns, no horns, spiked skin, talons for claws. Two were actually mages, if I had to guess. They looked human, at least. The attackers were standing in the road, but approached the sidewalk where we stood.

"Nix, run!" Ares shouted as he plunged his sword into the gut of the nearest demon.

Indecision tore at me, but only briefly. Though I *hated* to leave a fight, I couldn't let these jerks get the vessel of truth. Ares could handle them.

I spun toward P&P, sprinting toward the cafe. But a mage nearest me threw out his hands. A blast of wind hurtled over me, forming a shimmering barrier in front of me. I shielded my face with my arm and tried to plow through it, but I slammed into a solid wall.

Pain flared in my arm and I stumbled back.

Shit.

Running was out. I raised my sword and turned, taking stock. Ares was cutting down two demons while another two approached me.

I charged the nearest one, a demon with a wickedly curved sword and muscles that bulged out of the leather vest he wore. He raised his blade, but I parried, blocking his steel with my own. I kicked out, nailing him in the stomach. The breath whooshed out of him and I used his shock to plunge my blade into his neck.

Beside me, Ares swung his sword like a whirlwind, slicing through demons as if this was a game.

But it wasn't. More appeared, three in the street and one on the sidewalk. A mage conjured a fireball and hurled it at me. I swung my blade up, blocking the fireball, which exploded against the steel. Heat seared my face as sparks flew, singing my skin. The light from the flame blinded me.

A heavy arm wrapped around my waist, clutching tight. I lost my breath, plunging my blade backward blindly at the level of my waist. It sunk into flesh. A roar sounded at my ears as the arms around me loosened. I yanked away from my attacker.

My vision had finally cleared.

And we were *so screwed.*

Ares was cutting through demons left and right, but there

were still a dozen of them. *Bad* odds. And more were appearing every moment.

"Fire from above!" The voice sounded just as a fireball hurtled down from the sky, landing directly on the nearest demon's head. It flattened him, sending him to the pavement.

Across the street, the air shimmered, an opalescent sheen that was about the size of a car. For the briefest moment, my dragon sense tugged me toward it, then it was gone.

Weird.

Another demon charged me as an icicle flew down at him, piercing the skull of his nearest compatriot.

A quick glance overhead showed Cass and Del, hanging out of their windows and firing their magical weapons. Aidan leapt out of one window, transforming into a griffon on his way down. Golden magic swirled around him, dissipating to reveal a massive winged beast with a huge beak and fierce eyes. His feathers gleamed in the lamplight as he hurtled toward a demon on the ground. Roarke shifted midair as well, his back wings stretching wide as his demonic form appeared. He swept through the sky, aiming for the mage who was throwing fireballs.

I turned back to my attackers as two lunged toward me. Though I'd only looked skyward for half a second, it'd been enough time. One demon grabbed the box that I clutched to my chest, tearing it away. He yanked so hard that the leather strap snapped and I stumbled forward.

The thief dodged away as another came for me, blade raised. His flame-colored eyes blazed.

"Come on now," he growled.

CHAPTER THREE

Panic beat frantic wings within my chest as I swung my sword, desperate to cut him down so that I could rescue the beaker. He blocked my strike with his blade, then swept out with his massive claws. They raked across my side and stomach, sending pain flaring.

I gasped, biting back a cry and stabbing my sword toward his middle. He dodged, swiping out with his claws again. This time, I was faster, receiving only a shallow slice to my ribs. He growled his displeasure and I thrust my blade up into his gut.

His eyes widened and his mouth gaped. I kicked him in the middle, dislodging him from my sword. He fell backward and I turned from him, searching for more threats. Ares beheaded a demon while Aidan chomped one in two with his massive beak. I couldn't see Roarke, but assumed he was in the sky or behind me.

The thief who'd stolen the beaker wasn't far off, only ten feet away and dodging fireballs shot by Cass from above. I sprinted toward him, lungs burning and the wounds in my side aching with pain.

Another demon attacked me from the side, but a fireball landed on his head when he was only feet away. He roared as it flattened him to the ground. I dodged his flaming body, but another demon sprinted for me.

I had to get to that box! "Cass! Del! Backup!"

The demon who raced for me was only three feet away. I was about to swing with my sword—which would have been highly ineffective as I was still running after the demon who had stolen the box—when an icicle plunged through the top of his head. Del's weapon of choice.

Blood spurted and my stomach lunged at the grisly scene, but I turned back, racing for my prey.

"Go!" Cass shouted. "We've got your back!"

I sprinted harder. Demons came for me, but each was struck down by a fireball or icicle. Flesh burned and blood sprayed, an apocalypse of demon death all around me.

But I ignored it, trusting Del and Cass as I gained on my prey. He was dodging icicles sent by Del and doing a fabulous job of not getting hit, but they slowed him down enough that I caught up.

I plunged my blade into his back, stumbling with the force of my blow.

He staggered, roaring as he fell forward, and hit the ground with a heavy thud, the box clattering to the ground at his side. One of Cass's fireballs exploded against his back.

I scrambled forward, reaching for the box and clutching it near. A quick survey of the battle showed that the tide had turned.

We were winning.

Ares and Roarke were beheading their own demons while Ares sliced the neck of another. The rest were on the ground.

I hugged the box to my chest and grabbed the fallen demon's shoulder, dragging him onto his back. The cuts in my side screamed with pain and my blood dripped onto the sidewalk. I ignored it.

Where was the damned tattoo?

There had to be one. These had to be Drakon's men. I yanked at his high collar, pulling it back to reveal a tattoo of a writhing dragon, fangs bared and eyes gleaming.

Shit.

"They're Drakon's men!" I called. "Search the mages!"

My hands shook as I scavenged his pockets, searching for an ID or anything. But I wouldn't get lucky with a demon. They rarely carried ID. Someone would have to find one on a mage.

The demon's body began to crumble to dust. I cursed, stumbling back onto my butt. Normally, demon bodies took a little while to return to their underworld after they'd been killed. But anyone hired by Drakon seemed to be enchanted with a spell that poofed their bodies immediately.

He didn't want us tracking him. It was an effective method.

I scraped the flyaway hair from my face and dragged myself to my feet, clutching the box to my chest. My breath heaved as I leaned heavily against the wall, my wound and the fading adrenaline making me shake like a terrier in a thunderstorm.

All around me, the bodies of our attackers had turned to dust. Ares banished his shadow sword to the ether and strode toward me, a limp not slowing him down.

"Are you okay?" Concern darkened his voice.

"Fine." I gasped as pain flared in my side. A glance down revealed blood soaking through my blue T-shirt, coating the whole right side of my body. It'd traveled all the way up to the wiener dog who was sitting in a hotdog bun. "Shit."

"You aren't okay." Ares limped the last three feet toward me. My gaze went to his left thigh, where blood dripped down his leg.

"Maybe not quite." I sucked in shallow breaths, trying to control the pain.

Aidan landed with a thud next to us. He was so big that his beak was level with my head. Blood and gore smeared the smooth surface. Roarke landed next to him, dark gray skin speckled with blood that wasn't his.

"Drakon's men?" Roarke asked.

"Yes." I pressed a hand to the wound at my side, immediately cringing as pain flared. Right, bad idea. "Let's get inside."

Ares held out an arm, letting me lean on him. I got the sense he wanted to sweep me into his arms—that was a real Ares thing to do, I was learning—but that was a shitty idea with a wound like mine.

By the time we made it to the green door that was only fifteen feet away, the bodies of our attackers were no more than tiny piles of dust that would blow away on the wind.

I let us into the building and then made the laborious climb to my apartment door, grateful that I was on the first floor.

Del and Cass waited on the landing, faces pale and worried.

"Are you okay?" Cass asked.

"Yeah. Beaker is fine," I said.

"I meant you, dummy." She nodded to my wound. "That's ugly."

A wry grin twisted my mouth. "Thanks. Ruined my hot dog shirt."

"I'll get you a new one," Del said.

Cass pushed open my apartment door and held it open. I staggered through, dropping heavily onto the couch. My arms shook as I held up the box. "Check the beaker."

Del took it and the key I then handed her. She set the box on the coffee table and knelt, then unlocked the padlock and lifted the lid. A sigh escaped me at the sight of the unbroken beaker still nestled in its custom foam bedding. "Thank fates. They didn't get it."

Ares knelt at my side, his hand lifting my jacket away from the wound. "This is deep. Three claw marks."

"Are they poisoned?" Cass asked.

"Don't know." I gritted my teeth. "Burns like hell, though."

"I'll heal you." Ares raised a wrist to his mouth, ready to bite.

"No!" I held up a hand. "No, I've already had too much."

I was worried about the side effects from his blood. "Aidan, can you heal me?" His gifts came with no side effects.

"Yes." Aidan stepped forward.

Possessiveness—or something like it—flared in Ares's eyes and his knuckles whitened. His jaw hardened, as if he didn't like the idea of another man touching or healing me, but then he nodded and leaned back, a frown of resignation on his face. I reached for his hand. At least he could control his inner cave man.

Ares squeezed my hand, then released it and moved away so that Aidan could kneel at my side. His dark hair gleamed in the light as he leaned over me and hovered his hand over my wounds. Warmth flowed from his palm, soothing the burning ache until it faded to nothing. My muscles finally relaxed as the pain dissipated.

The lack of agony was pleasure in itself.

Aidan sat back. "That should do it."

I leaned up and peered at my side, nudged the torn shirt away until I could see that my flesh was once again unbroken. "Thanks."

"I don't think they were after the beaker," Del said.

My gaze darted to her. She still knelt by the box.

"What do you mean?"

"Even after the demon stole the box, all the rest kept going for you. It was easier to see the pattern from up above."

"I'm with Del," Cass said. "Drakon's men were after you, not the beaker."

"Well, maybe both," Del said. "But they were definitely after you."

I slumped back against the couch, my mind racing. "Damn."

"Why?" Ares demanded.

Del and Cass shrugged. "No idea."

I scrubbed a hand over my face. "Why now? Why me?"

"Maybe because you're the one who chased him up the stairs at his compound and made him evacuate?" Cass asked. "It's not the best theory, but it's all I've got right now."

"All I've got too," Del said. "He saw you, though. You were the biggest threat to him."

"Well, he now knows where we live," I said.

"How'd he find that out?" Ares asked.

"Powerful guy like him…" I said.

"But he can't get into the building," Cass said. "The protections are too strong."

"I'll stay the night with you," Ares said.

Pleasure flared in my chest at his words, followed quickly by worry.

After an injury like the one I'd just had, and as exhausted as I was, I wanted nothing more than to visit my trove. It was like a hunger inside me, something I couldn't ignore. And even though I trusted him, I couldn't invite him up there. Not yet.

My trove was private. The most personal thing in my life.

"Thank you, but not tonight. You already said you had to go back to the Vampire Court for something important. Do that. I'll be with these guys." I gestured to Cass and Del. "And no one can get in here, truly. We already had great security, and Aidan amped it up by a thousand a few months ago."

"I insist." He knelt by my side, eyes worried. That softness was such a contrast to the hardened shell that he always wore.

As much as I wanted to be with him—he was complex. My feelings for him were complex. The situation was freaking complex. And I needed to heal. To rest amongst my trove to get to one hundred percent strength.

Being with Ares… it certainly wasn't restful.

I had to be ready for whatever came at me. I didn't have time for distractions. Not now.

I reached for his hand, squeezing it. "Thank you. But go do

your business in the Vampire realm. It's important, right? And I'll be safe here."

His eyes flickered, indecision clearly warring within him. Finally, his mouth flat and his gaze resigned, he nodded. "I'll be back in the morning. Don't leave the apartment until I return."

I almost snapped at him that I knew how to take care of myself, but I bit my tongue. He meant well by it. I wouldn't make a habit of letting him tell me what to do, but right now, if it made him comfortable enough to give me the space I needed...

"Okay." I nodded, squeezing his hand once more. "Go do your thing."

He pressed a gentle kiss to my forehead, sending heat streaking through me at a most inappropriate time, then leaned down and whispered raggedly in my ear, "Be *careful*."

I sucked in a ragged breath and met his gaze. *Go. Don't go.*

I didn't know what to say.

But he saved me from that by standing and nodding to the others, then leaving.

I swallowed hard and turned to my friends. "Thanks for having our backs out there."

"Anytime." Concern shadowed Cass's eyes. "You need anything?"

"Just a shower and a nap. Then let's start fresh tomorrow."

"Well, you call us if you need us," Del said.

I smiled at her. "Always."

I didn't look in the mirror as I went into the bathroom to shower. The memory of the blood splattering on my face was enough to remind me that I didn't actually want to see my reflection.

Despite Aidan's healing ability, all my muscles ached as I leaned into the crummy old shower to crank on the water. Though my *deirfiúr* and I put vast quantities of loot into our troves, you'd never know it from the way our apartments looked.

As the shower heated up, I leaned my aching body against the small sink counter and stared at the box holding the beaker. I'd brought it into the shower for paranoia's sake, really, because once it was within the building, it was safe.

Mordaca was right. It was an unassuming thing, to be so powerful and coveted. Now I just had to figure out the potion that would allow me to use it. Because *damned* if I didn't want to understand the prophecy about dragons. Real dragons were supposed to be dead. Gone. So what did Drakon want with them? Whatever it was, I couldn't let him have it.

But we had so little to go on. Our clues were hardly even clues. Was I really capable of this? I knew so little about my past and my magic. My qualifications... Not impressive.

Suddenly, I realized that steam had filled the room and warmed my cheeks. I'd been staring at the beaker too long and wallowing in self-doubt. That would get me nowhere. I shoved the miserable thought away.

My muscles twinged as I shrugged out of my clothes and climbed into the water. Showering was a chore and the water ran pink—*gross*—but I was glad to finally be clean.

I was moving like a sloth by the time I shut off the water. As quickly as I could, which wasn't very quickly at all, I dried off and pulled on a fluffy robe.

With the box containing the beaker tucked under my arm, I climbed the stairs to my trove. It was only three flights up, but it felt like a hundred. Though my wound was closed, every inch of me hurt.

By the time I climbed up into the greenhouse, I was anxious to be amongst my treasures. It was more than my normal excitement over visiting my trove. This felt like a compulsion.

A *need* to be in my garden.

I shut the door behind me and turned to face my treasures.

The jungle spread out around me, plants sitting on tables and dangling from the ceiling. Vines and leaves and flowers filled the space, drinking the water that dripped from the custom irrigation system I'd installed. Whenever the water turned on, it felt like it was raining and I loved it.

Every muscle in my body relaxed just being here, loosening like I'd been to an hour-long massage. I grinned at the sight of my three cars, sitting on the other side of the jungle and out of reach of the sprinkler system. But it was the plants that called me this time.

I walked toward a table full of orchids. Their blooms were a riot of colors—pink, yellow, orange, white. It was strange, but as I walked, I almost felt stronger. As if some of the exhaustion and muscle aches from my wounds were fading.

The deep need that I'd had to be up here—the one that had made me banish Ares from the house—had settled somewhat, curling up in my chest like a snoozing kitten.

I set the box containing the beaker on the table, finding a space between two pots containing dragonfruit plants. Their thick green stalks supported strange red fruit that looked like something Dr. Seuss might have invented. I'd worked my butt off for this place, putting every penny I had into building my greenhouse.

I loved my plants. And I was almost sure they loved me. Even now, it seemed like the dragonfruit plants were leaning toward me.

I shook my head, trying to clear the image. That was too weird. Had to be the exhaustion. We'd been going straight for nearly two days after our last big sleep. I was due for a nap.

I strolled by the plants, running my fingertips over leaves and petals. It almost felt like energy flowed into me.

I made my way toward the Firebird, slipping inside the red car and leaning back against the seat to gaze out at my own personal paradise.

It wasn't long before my eyelids slid closed, lulled by the sense of rightness that I felt just being here. As I drifted in the hazy state between wakefulness and sleep, an errant thought tugged at my mind.

Something was up with my magic. Particularly around plants. I didn't know what it was, but something new seemed to be coming online…

∼

At first, I didn't realize that it was a dream.

I was back in the Monster's dungeon, in the lair of the man who'd stolen me away from my family. In the place where I'd first met Cass and Del, when we'd been so young. Children still, all of fourteen.

Too young for the horror of stone floors and walls that dripped with water. Too young for the echoes of the screams of those down the hall. Too young to be holed up in a place with no light and only rats for company.

But that didn't matter. I was back there anyway, unable to escape.

My heart thundered in my chest, an aching beat that hurt my ribs. Sweat chilled my skin despite the cool air of the dungeon. I gripped the stone floor upon which I sat, digging my fingernails into the crevices in the stone.

I was alone.

Cass and Del had not yet been brought here. Though I was within the dream, I was separate, watching. I tried to maintain that, to remain an observer, but I was dragged back into the mind of my fourteen-year-old self.

Dry sobs wracked my chest, but no tears poured from my eyes. I'd run out of tears long ago. Ever since they'd stolen me from my life, along with my mother and father. Weeks ago, a month? I had no idea. I'd lost track of time in this dark dungeon.

Come for me, Mum and Da.

But they couldn't hear my prayers. They'd have come if they could. They'd been stolen along with me—but they were so strong and fierce. Of course they could break free and come for me. They were my world. They could do *anything.*

Except it'd been so long. Ages that I'd been in the darkness, eating whatever gruel was shoved through the slot in the door. And my parents were nowhere to be seen. My strong, brave parents.

They weren't coming.

Since I'd been put in this room, I hadn't seen a single soul besides the guard who occasionally pushed food into the room.

Loneliness clawed at my chest. All I could hear was my own ragged breath, filling the horrible stone room where the men had thrown me.

I squeezed my eyes closed and tried to envision my home. Though it frightened me—how could I *not* be frightened of what was happening there?—I would give anything to return to my family and friends. It was better than this. Anything was better than this.

I curled in a ball against the stone wall, wishing for them with a ferocity that made my stomach ache. What had happened to them? Would they ever come for me? Would I ever be free?

CHAPTER FOUR

I woke with a start the next morning. Though there was a crick in my neck, the rest of my body felt rejuvenated and fresh. The nightmare that had haunted my dreams was a distant memory, leaving only a lingering sadness and fear.

For my old home? Why would I be afraid of my own home? Or so damned sad? It'd been like a quicksand pulling me down, a grief so deep I couldn't understand it. And I'd been so young when I'd been stolen away. How could a child feel so much?

Fates, I wished I had answers. Del and Cass had gotten theirs, learning about their pasts over the last year. But the mystery of my past still haunted me, an open wound that wouldn't heal.

But I had nothing. What I wouldn't give to learn what had happened to my family. I wanted it more than almost anything in the world.

Sun streamed through the glass roof, a shaft bright against my face. I blinked, thrusting away the sad memories and gazing out upon my trove. In the morning sun, the blooms blazed with light. It was one of my favorite times, when I could really see all the beauty that I'd worked so hard to create.

I climbed out of the car and collected the box containing the beaker. One last time, I ran my fingertips over the leaves and petals as I walked toward the staircase.

Though the sprinkler system would keep my plants alive, they needed some serious TLC soon. I loved pruning and trimming and fertilizing. Planting and sprouting and transferring. All of it fed my soul. But lately, I'd been so preoccupied with the task ahead of me that my garden had been faltering. My soul had been faltering. Even being away from the shop, my calm oasis in the madness of the world, was making me itchy.

If I wanted to get back to any of this, I needed to finish this and take down Drakon. Or I'd never get my life back.

I took the stairs two at a time, descending to my apartment.

I showered quickly, then dressed in my usual motorcycle boots and jeans, topping it with a vintage Wonder Woman T-shirt. Just as I was tugging on my jacket and dreaming of a coffee from P&P, a pebble clattered against my window.

Ares.

He still didn't have access to the green door that allowed entrance to the building. I went to the window to check, grinning when I saw him standing on the sidewalk. He held a small package in his hand.

I gave him a thumbs-up, then grabbed the beaker box and slipped the strap over my head. I'd had to conjure a new strap and had been sure to make this one extra thick.

Rejuvenated from my R&R, I took the stairs two at a time. At the bottom, I pushed open the door and stepped out into the cool morning air. Ares stood about ten feet down the sidewalk, talking to a man I didn't recognize. I turned toward them, the box clutched to my chest, memories of the attack last night still fresh in my mind.

Ares turned toward me, a smile in his eyes.

Out of the corner of my eye, the air shimmered with an opalescent sheen. It pulled at me, a magnet. Time slowed as I turned toward it, every second stretching to a minute. I felt every molecule in the air against my skin, heard the slowed-down chirping of the birds. But my gaze was fully riveted on the shimmering air in front of me.

Hunger yawned inside me. It had to be a portal.

My dragon sense tugged *hard* toward the gateway, the fiercest it'd ever been.

My mind zeroed in on one fact—answers lay within. So many answers to questions I'd held for so long. How I knew that, I had no idea. But I *did*.

Maybe it was my dragon sense, which was screaming for me to step into the portal. I'd never wanted anything so badly in all my life. It consumed me, forcing away thoughts of the beaker, Drakon, my life on earth.

This was what I wanted.

So I did it, stepping into the shimmering light.

Immediately, the world went wild around me. Wind and rain and snow and hot summer air buffeted me as trees and oceans and deserts shimmered in the distance. It was everything at once, and I was spinning through it like a top.

This was nothing like transporting, which was always dark. This was a sensory explosion that short-circuited my mind. I tried to scream, but the vacuum of space stole the breath straight from my lungs.

A second later, the portal ejected me, throwing me onto the ground. The air whooshed out of me as the box dug into my gut, my vision going temporarily blind while I adjusted to the dim light after the brightness of the portal.

I blinked, scrambling upright with the box clutched to my chest.

Where the heck was I? And had I really just stepped into that portal?

But it had promised me answers. Wordlessly, but it had promised all the same.

I spun in a circle, taking in my surroundings as my muscles tensed and my magic readied for defense. I was in a silent forest.

A terrifying forest.

The trees were dead—skeletal white and black oaks that had no leaves. They stretched as far as the eye could see, dotting the landscape around me. Beneath my feet, there was no grass, just dirt.

The sun was low in the sky—morning, I guessed. But the signs of life that I'd expect to see in a forest were all gone.

It was a graveyard.

A brief sense of déjà vu hit me. An old man in this forest. Then it was gone as if it'd never existed.

I swallowed hard, my eyes darting around for any sign of life or even a threat. There was an eerie chill on the air, something that explicitly said *This is not right.*

Beneath my feet, I could feel a slow thudding, so light that it almost wasn't there. I took a few hesitant steps toward one of the dead trees, horrified by the state it was in.

Tentatively, I touched the bark. Again, I swore I felt a slow thud beneath my palms.

What the heck was that?

Magic sparked at my back, a signature that felt like tiny bubbles in water.

I turned, braced for anything.

A woman stood about twenty feet away. A ghost or spirit of some kind.

My breath grew shallow as I inspected her.

She was pale white, nearly transparent. Her long dress flowed to her feet and her hair was strange, almost as if it were made of leaves. I'd never seen her before—that, I was sure of.

Despite her magical signature, very little power radiated from her. Still, my hair stood on end. It wasn't every day I ran into a ghost.

"Who are you?" I asked.

She didn't answer, just glided closer to me. As she neared, I realized that her eyes sparkled.

I tried another question. "Where am I?"

"Home." Her voice was whispery, almost like the wind.

"Um, I'm not." I glanced around at all the dead trees. This was so not my home. It couldn't be.

She gestured. "Come with me."

"Where?"

She didn't answer, just glided away. I had no other answers, no other ideas. But I needed to be here. The sense was so strong that I couldn't ignore it. I just needed to figure out why.

So I followed her.

"Why is this place dead?" I asked.

She glanced at me, eyes sparkling. "It isn't my story to tell."

"Will you take me to the one who can?" *Take me to your leader.* I sure wasn't a little green man, but I did want to find someone who would answer my questions.

Why had I been drawn here?

She led me through the forest for ten minutes. When a few buildings appeared through the trees on my left, I pointed. "Can we go there?"

"That is not the way." She glided along, her magic sparkling against my skin. Whenever she passed a tree, it seemed to glow just slightly. Then it faded.

I was about to demand more answers when we reached a clearing. On my left, there was a tall, shimmering white barrier. Just like the portal I'd entered, but it was enormous. To the right, the dead trees thinned to form a courtyard.

I turned to inspect it more fully and my jaw dropped.

"Whoa," I murmured, awe spreading through me.

Across the courtyard, which was at least two hundred meters long, a village climbed up a valley between two tall mountains that loomed on either side. The buildings themselves crowded against one another, all situated around a central street that rose up the valley ridge.

The mountains were a spectacular backdrop to the village, peaks rising tall on either side of the main street. They were made of golden brown stone, shot through with veins of glittering amber. Waterfalls poured from crevices along the ridges, disappearing down into the valley behind the village.

Holy crap, it looked like freaking Themyscira. I'd swear that Wonder Woman was going to jump off one of those buildings at any minute.

Except that it was *dead*. Despite all the water, there was no greenery. Not a single leaf or tree or flower or blade of grass. Not in the village nor on the mountains.

It wasn't just one dead forest—there wasn't a single living plant anywhere. The lack of life here sent grief through me, a weight that pulled at my heart. It was followed quickly by a ghost of fear. It was more like a residual emotion—one I'd once felt here.

"What happened here?"

The woman pointed toward the village. "You'll find your answers there."

I turned to her, but she was already drifting away, back to the dead forest. I debated only briefly, then hurried across the courtyard.

Though I didn't know where to find answers, my dragon sense sure had some ideas. It tugged toward the main street, so I followed. On my left, there was a row of buildings, like they'd been put there to take advantage of the once-nice courtyard. But most of the buildings rose up the valley ridge ahead of me, so steep it was almost cartoonish. How did people live here?

I saw a few people through windows of their houses, but I didn't bother to knock on their doors. Unlike the ghostly woman, these people were alive and well. My dragon sense led me toward the central part of town.

When I reached the main street, I was at the bottom end of the village, looking up a road that climbed high into the mountains. Ancient buildings made of beautiful beige stone crowded it on both sides, and fountains poured water into basins at regular intervals. Terra-cotta roofs lent it a magical air.

The buildings were pressed right up against each other, all sharing walls. Some were shops, others were homes. No technology marred the ancient beauty here, as if it'd been trapped away from time and change. A hidden kingdom.

I stepped onto the street and began to climb, desperate to figure out what the heck was going on and why my dragon sense was so excited to be here. It was early enough that no one was out on the street yet, though I caught flashes of people through windows. Their clothes were simple, and definitely not modern. Sort of Medieval, with tunics and the like.

Why the hell had I felt so compelled to come here? My mind whispered that this might actually be my home. That the weird ghost lady was right.

I might be on the path to some answers. My heart thudded, excitement flowing through my veins. If this was my home, my parents might be here. Hope filled me with light, but I tried to shove it away. I had no idea if they were alive. I didn't want to be crushed if I were wrong.

But this place was so *dead.* How could it be my home? I loved plants. I was Life in the Triumvirate, whatever that really meant.

This couldn't be my home.

The only plants here were flowers and vines carved into the fountains that flowed out of the walls of the old buildings. Stone arches that spread over the top of the street were carved with flowers as well.

Though it was fabulously beautiful with the stone and amber and waterfalls, it was wrong somehow. My hair stood on end. Even my body sensed that something was off here.

I climbed past a few more houses, headed to I didn't even

know where. As I walked, déjà vu started to hit me hard. I'd been here before, hadn't I? Or not?

Damn, this sucked. My mind spun as I tried to make sense of this place.

"Stop!" A commanding voice came from behind.

I turned, heart in my throat. The largest man I'd ever seen—he had to be nearly seven feet tall—stood about ten feet away from me, a sword drawn and his leather armor gleaming in the morning sun. Light glinted off metal discs sewn onto the leather.

I could have drawn my bow—met his threat with one of my own. But I didn't.

Sometimes, in the movies, there's a moment where the character realizes something huge has happened. They just stand there and watch, understanding that the world is changing around them. Like Neo in the Matrix. I was Neo, and I was about to take the red pill.

"Where am I?" I asked.

Confusion creased his brow. "You are trespassing."

"Not sure about that. A portal appeared to me—felt a hell of a lot like an invitation."

Surprise flared in his brown eyes. Then they hardened. "Come with me."

"Where are you taking me?"

"To the head steward. She will determine what to do with you."

"Is she in charge?"

"While the queen and king are away, yes."

"All right then, let's go." They could throw me in a dungeon, kill me for trespassing, use me for archery practice—who knew? But I wanted answers, and my dragon sense was clear—there were answers in this place. It'd never led me wrong before and I didn't think it was about to start.

"Good." He almost looked surprised at my lack of fuss, but I didn't have time to dillydally around.

He led me up the street toward a large building on the left. It looked almost like a municipal building, except that it had fabulous stone architecture and was probably about a thousand years old.

"What is this place called?" I asked as he gestured me inside the building.

"Elesius. But the steward will answer your questions." He led me into a fabulous library.

Shelves of books surrounded me, leather spines lined up neatly. Comfy chairs were scattered about the large room, along with tables and a desk. Light shined in from a glass ceiling, along with windows high on the walls. Colorful glass lamps sat on surfaces, but the candles within were not lit.

"Wait here." Morpheus left. Even though he hadn't handed me the red pill himself, the nickname fit.

I explored the room, finding books I'd never heard of. The door creaked open behind me, a noise so slight I almost didn't hear it.

I turned. A woman entered, shock sending her brows up to her hairline. Her dress was long and pale green, her hair a riot of red and gray curls around her face. She wasn't my mother, but she was vaguely familiar.

The woman spread her arm out. "Phoenix Lividius, you are home."

Chills raced over my skin. "What do you mean? How do you know my name?"

Footsteps sounded from the hall behind her. My eyes darted to the empty space in the doorway. Morpheus appeared.

"This is your home, Phoenix Lividius." the woman smiled. "We've been searching for you."

My home.

Something familiar pulled at my mind. My gaze darted around the room, taking in the books and the chairs and the windows streaming light that made the dust motes sparkle.

I was home? Could my parents possibly be here?

Joy and fear ricocheted through me, a lightness and a heaviness that didn't know how to coexist inside one body. I searched my mind for more memories, but none came.

There were types of mind manipulation magic—Doyen's had screwed with me enough that I was too intimately familiar. But this didn't feel like that.

"I'm from here?"

"Yes. I'm Moira." She gestured to Morpheus. "That is Orion. He is a guard. I am consul to your mother, the queen."

"Is she alive?" My heart leapt. "My father?"

I had only the vaguest memories of them, gleaned from nightmares of the Monster using them against me. They'd been abducted along with me, according to my sparse memories.

"They are alive." A tentative smile pulled at Moira's lips. "They are on a trading expedition. One that could not wait. But we've sent word. They will be home soon."

My head felt like a balloon, floating among the clouds. *My parents were alive.*

"I'm home." The words felt foreign and strange.

"Yes." Moira gestured for me to come forward. "Come, I'll show you to your room."

"What is this place? The library?"

"My personal study. As well as being consul to your mother, I'm the steward in Elesius. While your parents are gone, I act in their stead."

"Okay." I looked at Orion, the solemn giant who stood at her side. I still liked the name Morpheus better, but I was sure he wouldn't get the joke. "What is this place?"

"We are a kingdom, cut off from the world by magic," Moira said.

"Like another realm?" I'd already had enough with the Vampire Realm.

"Not exactly." Moira gestured. "Come. I will take you to your room so that you can freshen up. Your mother will be here soon."

My mother. That sounded crazy.

Could this really be true? I believed her. I *wanted* to believe her. I'd been missing my family so badly for so long. The not-knowing was one of the hardest parts. And now there were answers.

"Okay, let's go." I clutched the box and walked over to join her.

Moira nodded and led us from the room. Orion stayed at her side and I trailed behind.

"This way." Moira led me up the main street, which was just as beautiful—and barren—as the lower part of the city.

"Why are there no plants?" I asked. "It's terrible."

"That is not my story to tell." Moira gestured. "Come."

She repeated Morpheus's earlier words, which was odd. I tucked that bit of info away for later.

"Has this place been cursed?" There was a sadness here, and that darkness I'd felt earlier.

"I cannot say." Moira's gaze shuttered.

A shimmer to my left caught my eye. A short alleyway diverted off the main street. It dead-ended at a glimmering opalescent wall. Just like the large wall at the base of the city, near the courtyard.

"What's this?" I started toward it, hoping it was a portal. I'd need a way out of here when it was time to go.

"Don't!" Moira's voice was sharp.

A hand grabbed my arm, strong and sure.

I spun, striking Orion's arm. "Let go!"

He dropped his hand, stepping back. Moira rushed forward. "It's nothing. It's just the barrier between here and the rest of the world. But you cannot leave." Desperation filled her eyes.

"Cannot?" Annoyance seethed in my chest.

"No, you cannot. It'd be—" She drew in a shuddering breath. "You just cannot. You are home. You cannot leave."

She meant it. Her eyes were fierce, her cheeks flushed.

Ah, shit. This was going to be a problem.

There was something very weird about this place and the inhabitants telling me I couldn't leave.

I spun, racing away from her, toward the wall. I had to test it —had to see.

They didn't follow me, which should have been my first indicator. I stopped right before the barrier and thrust my hand toward it. An electric shock drove me backward, I crashed to the ground, pain singing through my back. I barely managed to keep my grip on the wooden box.

Shit.

I scrambled to my feet, spinning to face them. Moira's eyes were unreadable. So were Orion's. "You knew that would happen."

"We tried to stop you," Moira said.

"You cannot keep me prisoner here." Even if it was my home, and my parents were here, I couldn't *stay* here. I had a life to live. A battle to fight.

Had I walked into a trap?

"You aren't a prisoner." The words rushed out of Moira. "You aren't."

"Kinda feels like I am."

"You aren't!" She shook her head, gaze a bit manic.

Moira was not holding it together well, and something was definitely weird. Orion was a statue next to her, his face completely unreadable.

"Will my parents be back soon?" I asked.

"Yes." She nodded, grasping the lifeline of a change in topic. "Come, come. I'll show you to your room."

I followed Moira out of the alley and back down the street, taking in the people and architecture, all of which were foreign yet familiar.

She led me to a large building in the middle of town. The

sculptures decorating the structure were magnificent. Vines and leaves and trees so lifelike they only lacked color to appear real.

"This is where you live," she said.

"Lived."

"Of course." She took me through a room that was decorated with colorful paintings and up a set of stairs to a medium-sized chamber featuring a bed, a couch, and a dresser. "This is your room."

It was familiar, in the way that dreams could be. "Thank you."

She left me.

Immediately, I pressed my fingertips to the charm around my neck, igniting the magic. "Cass? Del? You there?"

I got nothing. The magic was blocked by the barrier.

Not a surprise. But it sucked.

I put the box containing the beaker on the bed and spun in a circle, taking in the space. No memories came. Damn the spell that had taken my memory. It'd saved us from the Monster, but the trauma of so much magic had stolen our memories. Now, even my childhood bedroom was a mystery.

Moira had called me Phoenix Lividius. *Phoenix.* When I'd woken in the field at fifteen, I'd given myself that name, thinking that I'd chosen it from the constellation above. Except it had always been my name. I smiled.

Lividius, though. I'd forgotten that. Frankly, I preferred my chosen last name of Knight.

Voices sounded from below. Eerily familiar ones.

I ran to the window, shoving it open and leaning out. Below, two figures in their fifties were dismounting from enormous horses. They were both dressed in the same leather armor as Orion had been. A man and a woman.

My mother and father.

A gasp strangled in my throat and my head swam. *My mother and father. Mum and Da!*

CHAPTER FIVE

They were real. They were alive. And I recognized them. Even from up here, I could see my mother's brown hair and green eyes. My father's dark hair and tall build. I was about to wave when they raced inside.

Holy fates! Excitements and nerves collided inside me. I didn't know how to process this. They were here!

Would they like me?

Oh, shit, this was bad.

I had no more time to worry. My mother burst through the door, her brown hair flying behind her.

Shock and joy stole my breath as she collided with me, throwing her arms around me. "Phoenix!"

Her voice was so familiar. Even though I hadn't remembered it until now, it was familiar. Tears burned my eyes. I clutched her to me, amazed that I was finally with my mother again. This was *real.*

My father joined us, wrapping his arms around the two of us. Joy like I'd never known filled my body.

My parents.

I'd wanted them for so long. Wanted answers. And here they were.

My mother pulled back, tears sparkling in her green eyes. "Let me look at you."

I smiled, tears pouring down my face.

"You're so beautiful. And so big." She looked at my father. "We've lost so many years."

"But we've found her." His gray gaze met mine. "We've found you."

"How?"

"Come." My mother held my hand, gesturing toward the door. "We'll go to the sitting room."

I collected the beaker and followed them to a room with two couches and a fireplace. Finally, a memory rushed to the surface. Me, playing here as a child.

We sat on the couches, my mother next to me and my father on the other couch. There was a massive window in front of me showing a beautiful view of the city and mountains. I turned toward my mother.

"How did the portal finally appear to me after so long?"

She reached for my hand. Only then did I realize that not only was she dressed like a warrior, she looked like one. Her arms were strong and lean, daggers sheathed at her hips.

"We've been searching ever since you were captured on one of our trading expeditions to the outside world," my mother said. "He took us as well, but we escaped within the first day. We tried to find you, but they'd taken you elsewhere. We've searched ever since, but you were well hidden."

Tears pricked my eyes. At least they'd searched for me. And I wasn't responsible for my father's death—he wasn't even dead. The Monster's threat had been empty, the vision of my father being run through by a sword was an illusion. My shoulders relaxed, as if for the first time in my life. Like I'd been carrying that tension and that fear for a decade.

"It's taken ten years." My father frowned. "Too long."

"Why now?" I asked.

"In the last week, your unique magical signature has grown. Our tracker could sense that. Finally, we had a way to find you, and our strongest wizard sent a portal to you. It was drawn to you by your unique magic."

"My unique magic? You mean my FireSoul nature?"

"No." My mother shook her head. "I mean your gift over life. Over plants."

So I wasn't crazy.

"You would have learned your magic sooner if you'd been here," my mother said. "But the magic waited, bursting free when it couldn't wait any longer."

"I wouldn't call it bursting," I said. "Some strange stuff has happened with plants. But no bursting."

Should there have been bursting?

My mother laughed. "It will come."

"Why do I have such great plant magic if this place has no plants at all?" Despite my parents' arrival, it still felt strange here. Wrong, somehow.

My mother and father shared a look, indecision and worry.

"What is it?" I demanded.

"We must tell her," my father said.

"Not yet." My mother whispered, worry in her gaze.

"Tell me what?" The hair on my arms stood on end.

"It's nothing," my mother said. "It can wait until—"

"Tell me." I gripped her hands. "Please."

Resignation shined in her eyes, and that scared me more than anything.

"Fine." She swallowed hard, then gestured to the huge glass window that gave a fabulous view of the city climbing up the valley and the mountains towering overhead. "It's beautiful, isn't it?"

"It is."

"It was once covered in greenery. Plants and trees and crops in the lower valley beyond."

"What happened?"

"You were born."

Uh, that sounded *bad.*

"But it was a good thing," she rushed to say. "A good thing. Though this place began to die. The plants and trees slowly withering away, giving their life and their magic to you."

Horror opened a cavern in my chest. "That's terrible."

"It's not." My mother smiled. "It was fated to be this way. *You* were fated to be. Elesius was created to birth *Life.* To create you, who would in turn use the magic to defeat a great evil."

Holy fates, this was what the prophecy meant when it said that I represented Life in the Triumvirate. "Is this why this place feels so strange? And why I feared it as a child?"

"Yes." My mother nodded. "You knew it was dying, but didn't understand why. It scared you."

I scrubbed a hand over my face, my thoughts whirring. "Why me?"

I wasn't strong enough for this. Wasn't worthy of the sacrifice made by Elesius.

My mother smiled. "Because you're the one with the will to do what must be done. Elesuis knew this was our fate—a seer decried it long ago. *Life* would come from my line, which is why I am queen."

Oh, man. I hoped that didn't mean I'd be made queen. I did not need that on my plate.

"But it wasn't me, nor any of my ancestors," my mother said. "When you were born, it was like Elesius knew the time had come. And it began to die."

"Giving me its power." Holy fates, this was *awful.* My stomach churned.

"You are the Warrior of Elesius," my father said. "The princess of our kingdom. Fated to defeat the evil that rises."

"This has been in the works for thousands of years." My mother gripped my hand. "But I didn't want you to have to face this."

It was suddenly hard to breathe. "When you say that I'm supposed to fight—"

A flash of movement in the window caught my eye. A figure crashed through, glass exploding into the room. He moved as fast as lightning, streaking toward me and grabbing me, dragging me toward the wall.

It was a blur as he positioned himself in front of me and held out a dark blade toward my parents.

Recognition slammed into me.

"Ares!" I shoved him, but he wouldn't budge.

"Step back," Ares commanded of my parents. "Don't come near her."

Oh shit, he was rescuing me. *Of course* he was rescuing me.

My mother drew her daggers, looking like a serious bad-ass Amazon, while my father drew his sword.

"Step away from her," my mother demanded.

I wiggled out from behind Ares. "It's okay, everyone. It's okay."

"It's not," my father said. "He's entered our kingdom. That should be impossible."

He clearly didn't know Ares. Though I had no idea how Ares had found me or gotten here, that wasn't top of my list right now. Brokering a ceasefire took precedence.

I reached for Ares's arm, noting the tensed muscles and warrior's gleam in his eyes. "Ares. Meet my parents."

His shock was so brief I almost didn't see it. But the flickering of his eyelids gave it away.

I turned to my parents. "Mother and Father, meet my…" What was he to me? I had no idea yet. "Ares. Meet Ares."

Who had my back.

No question now.

"I'm certain everyone can lower their blades," I said.

"You don't remember your parents," Ares said.

"I do now."

His gaze traveled from my parents to me, and then back again. "They aren't affiliated with Drakon?"

"That was my thought, but no." I pushed on his arm.

He lowered his sword. My parents followed suit.

Ares looked at me, face intense. "Are you all right?"

"I'm fine. Shaken up, but fine." I was about to ask him about the burn on his cheekbone when my father spoke.

"How did you get in here?" he demanded.

"I can cross realms." He turned to me. "Your *deirfiúr* tried to come but they could not cross over."

"What are *deirfiúr*?" my mother asked.

I opened my mouth to tell her about the family I'd created after I'd been stolen from them, but Moira rushed into the room, panic on her face.

"There's been a breach." Moira's eyes were stark. "In the lower city."

My parent's eyes darted to Ares. "Is that where you came from?"

He shook his head. "I came from the higher end of the city. In the mountains."

"We must go." My mother looked at me. "Stay here."

"No way in hell."

Frustration twisted her face. "Then be careful."

This was all in a day's work for me, but I doubted any loving mother wanted to hear that her kid fought demons on the daily. So I just said, "Okay."

She and my father raced out of the room. I grabbed the box from the coffee table and followed, Ares at my side. At the door, he grabbed my arm, pulling me to a halt.

"What?"

He dug into his coat pocket, dragging out the package he'd

been holding while standing beneath my window. He tore into the brown paper, revealing a cuff bracelet that flamed purple and red. He shoved it toward me. "Put it on."

"What is it?"

"Protection. Put it on."

I shoved it onto my wrist. It was large enough that I had to push it up onto my bicep to keep it from coming off. Magic sparked through me, like a shield had drifted around me.

I wanted to ask what the hell it was, but Ares had started running after my parents.

"Are attacks normal here?" Ares asked as we raced down the cobblestone street behind my parents.

"No idea." I looped the leather strap over my shoulders and sprinted harder. I'd made it my mission to not let the beaker out of my sight until I'd harnessed its magic, but it was becoming a real pain in the butt.

People spilled out of houses and shops, running alongside us down the street. They were armed with blades and bows, and dressed in similar old-timey armor like my parents.

It was surreal, to be rushing to the defense of my homeland alongside people I may have known as a child. My heart thundered, joy and fear twined together.

The main street terminated in the courtyard where I'd entered. Ahead, it stretched about two hundred meters toward the gleaming opalescent barrier. There were a few skeletal trees that I now realized had given their life for mine. Their power for mine.

A hundred meters in the distance, the shimmering white veil that protected this place was torn asunder. Figures were spilling forth, racing toward the town's inhabitants.

My parents sprinted across the courtyard, hurtling toward the demons. A line of buildings extended along the right side of the courtyard.

"I'm going up high." I shifted the box so it hung off my back.

"Be careful." He left, running toward the fight.

I ran for the row of houses along the courtyard, jumping onto a windowsill and scrambling up onto the roof. I conjured a bow —old faithful. Once I'd found purchase on the tiles, I knelt, firing an arrow at a demon who was about to collide with my mother. She had her daggers ready and a warrior's stance, ready to slice the demon to ribbons, but my arrow thudded into his right eye just before he reached her.

She spun, her gaze finding me on the roof. A grin spread across her face. I smiled back.

It was weird, bonding over battle, but it was my kind of weird.

She turned back to the fray, daggers ready. At her side, my father swung a massive sword, taking the head off a demon with the biggest horns I'd ever seen.

I fired my arrows, taking out a lightning mage who'd barely missed striking a woman with a spear.

Ares cut through the battlefield, taking out enemy after enemy. My parents and Ares, along with the other villagers, had it covered on the ground. In the distance, I spotted a mage standing near the tear in the barrier. His hands were outstretched toward the rip. Magic glowed from his palms and streaked toward the tear.

He was keeping it open while attackers continued to pour through.

I drew a steadying breath and sighted my arrow, then fired toward my target. The arrow whistled through the air, straight and true.

Until it was incinerated by a fire mage standing between me and my target. The blast of flame streaked through the air, devouring the slender wooden shaft in an instant.

Shit.

I conjured another arrow and shot at the fire mage, knowing it was likely hopeless. And it was. He blasted the arrow to bits before it ever reached him.

I'd never get to the guy holding open the barrier this way. But Ares wasn't too far away. He'd just removed both arms from a demon with claws made of flame. One last blow of his shadow sword beheaded the beast.

"Ares!" I called.

He turned to me. I pointed toward the fire mage and called. "Get him!"

Ares shifted, turning toward the mage. He sprinted toward the man, his vampire speed eerie in its grace. I took off across the rooftop, scrambling onto the next and leaping onto the one after. I needed to get closer to the mage. He was protected by the line of attackers who stood between me and him, but if I could come at him laterally…

I felt like Batman as I leapt over rooftops and skidded along tile. Finally, I neared the barrier, which shimmered with a pale opalescent light.

The portal mage—or whatever he was—had his back toward me as he directed his magic at the tear in the barrier. It crackled with electric light.

I knelt and sighted my arrow, focusing on his back as I released the string. The arrow whistled through the air, colliding with his broad back. And then bounced off.

What the hell?

My arrows flew with enough force to pierce most armor, and this guy was wearing just a shirt. I conjured another arrow and aimed for his neck. It flew straight and true, but he dodged out of the way right before it struck.

It plowed into the barrier, shattering.

Damn.

But at least his focus was broken. The portal closed without his magic to sustain it. I leapt off the building, conjuring a sword as I raced toward the mage.

He was tall and young—not much older than I—but his magic stank like week-old tuna left out in the sun. As much as I loathed killing, this guy was just plain evil. His magical signature was a flag, declaring it for the world.

And he'd opened the portal into this peaceful world, bringing death and destruction.

I was ten feet from him when he threw out his hands and blasted his magic toward me. The crackling white light streaked through the air. I dodged, diving left, and narrowly avoided it. He was fast though, and the second blast hit me straight in the midsection, bowling me backward.

Pain flared as I crashed to the ground. The box strapped to me dug into my back before shifting to my side so I lay flat. It felt like stepping on a giant Lego. I sucked in a ragged breath, the shock of the blow keeping me pinned to the dirt. Stunned, I craned my neck to see my opponent. The mage was striding toward me, hands glowing as he charged up another blow.

Thank fates he wasn't strong enough to strike three times simultaneously.

I played possum as pain wracked me, lying still and weak on the ground as strength flowed back into my body. I had the errant thought that if this place had any plant-life left, I'd be able to draw strength from them.

But Elesius had already given me everything it had.

Tears pricked the back of my eyes, but I dared not let them fall. Now was the time for battle, not grief.

The mage stomped over, looming over me, features twisted with rage. He held out his hands, glowing with light.

"Don't kill her!" The rough shout came from twenty feet away. Another mage. "She's the target!"

The words just pissed me off. Indecision flickered in the mage's eyes as he stood over me. I used that second's hesitation to thrust my sword upward, aiming for his gut.

But he dodged, narrowly avoiding my blade, and grabbed my arm roughly.

Magic exploded out from me, blasting the mage onto his ass

five feet away. Shock flared. What the hell? It felt like it came from the bracelet that Ares had given me, but I'd never experienced anything like that.

I scrambled to my feet, my aches fading, and lunged for the mage. He leaned on one arm, the other extended out to me, light flaring from his palm.

I was about to charge him when something silver flew by, headed straight for him. A dagger thudded into the mage's chest. His eyes flared with shock.

I glanced back. My mother stood ten meters away, having just thrown one of her daggers. She'd saved me.

A grin spread across my face. I nodded at her, then turned and ran for the mage, who was bleeding out onto the ground.

"Bitch," he spat, blood burbling from his lips.

"Not gonna argue there."

His eyes went still a moment later, dark and lifeless. A tinge of grief struck me for the life that was lost. He was evil, but he hadn't always been so.

I knelt at his side, pushing back his collar.

The dragon tattoo twisted over his collarbone. It was no surprise, but my shoulders sagged anyway.

Buck up, buttercup. There was a battle to be won.

I surged to my feet, turning to face the field. Ares stood over the body of the man who'd shouted that I was the target. And my mother's people—my people—had turned the battle toward victory. My mother and father were polishing off the last demons. The rest were scattered on the ground, already disappearing.

Ares strode toward me, eyes intense and face speckled with blood. "Are you all right?"

"Yeah." I winced as I shifted the box strapped to my back. This stupid thing was becoming seriously awkward. And even though it was safe inside its specially designed foam padding, there was always the chance that something could happen to it. Fire ball, lightning—anything was possible. I needed to get this back to my trove ASAP.

"They're Drakon's men," Ares said.

"Yeah." I hiked a thumb toward the mage, who'd already turned to dust. "That one had the tattoo."

There was no question about it—Drakon was after me. Somehow, he was powerful enough to track me all the way here. I'd gotten lucky both times, being surrounded by friends and family who had my back. But eventually, my luck would run out.

And then?

Well, I didn't know what would happen then. But it'd be the fight of my life.

CHAPTER SIX

An hour later, after my mother and father had seen to the wounded and the five who had died, we gathered around a table filled with food imported from the outside world. That was one of the many downsides of me taking all the plant-life from Elesius, and guilt was heavy in my stomach.

We were in a small dining room in my parents' house, a space that vaguely reminded me of childhood meals. Ares sat at my side, my parents across from us.

I swallowed a bite of potatoes covered in cheese and looked at my parents. "I'm sorry about those who died."

My mother's gaze met mine. "Don't be. We are all prepared to defend our home."

"But they were after me."

My mother sighed, her eyes heavy with worry. "I was afraid of that. It has begun, hasn't it? The great evil you are meant to fight?"

"Yes." My appetite was waning. I explained what I knew of Drakon.

"He must be powerful if he made it through our barrier." My

father shook his head. "That has not happened in centuries. Now twice in one day."

"But I didn't come to wage war," Ares said.

"Yes you did." My mother smiled. "Fortunately, you didn't need to."

Ares nodded.

"This Drakon is your fate, then," my mother said. "The reason Elesius died."

I swallowed hard. I was always the sidekick, never the hero. And now a whole kingdom had died to give me the power I needed to win the battle?

Oh, man.

"Do you know your next step?" my father asked. "We will help you."

I picked up the box from the floor and removed the beaker, then held it up. "I'm going to use this to untangle the prophecy. Then I'll know what he's after, and hopefully be able to stop him. The knowledge could even lead me to him."

My mother's eyes flared wide. "Where did you get that?"

"A tomb in northern England. Do you recognize it?"

She nodded slowly. "I do. And I cannot say that I am surprised."

She held out her hands and I passed it across the table. She studied the incised decoration, tracing her fingers over the carvings. "This was made by the immortal wizard Ademius. He was one of us, long ago. An ancestor of ours who used his magic to extend his life. His name and deeds have passed through the ages."

Ademius. The name tugged at a memory, but I couldn't place it. "Could I maybe find where he went?"

"You're meant to find him," my father said. "It's no coincidence that you were chosen for this, Nix. You are the Warrior of Elesius, created by our world. Given the tools to fight this battle."

My mother swallowed hard, tears glinting in her eyes. "I'd hoped you wouldn't have to face this."

I reached across the table, gripping her hand. "It's okay."

"It's not. But it is what it is." She looked at my father, who nodded. "Before Ademius left, he knew that the Warrior of Elesius would have to seek him out. The seer told him so. He left something to help you track him."

My heart leapt. It was going to be hard enough to find a guy who was thousands of years old—or dead—but at least I'd have a clue.

~

Later that evening, after showering in a little stone room with a fountain shaped like a lotus, there was a knock on my bedroom door.

"Come in." I finished tugging on my boots and stood. It was only eight p.m., but I wanted to go find Ares.

My mother stepped inside, two small boxes clutched in her hands. "How are you?"

"Fine." I didn't think *scared* or *feeing unworthy* would go over well, so I stuck with fine.

"Fine never means fine."

Of course my mother saw right through me.

"It might, if I keep telling myself that."

She smiled and took my hand, then sat on the bed. I followed her down. "You are strong Nix. You can do this. You were born to do this, and I believe in you."

My mother believed in me. It was something that should be obvious, but I'd been without her for so long that just hearing the words were a balm on my soul. And they helped, somehow. They erased a tiny bit of the doubt that I felt. I squeezed her hand. "Thank you."

"That vampire is handsome." Her green eyes sparkled.

"He is." My heart fluttered.

The sparkle in her eyes faded. "Be careful, though. He is death, and you are life. Opposites."

"Opposites attract." I frowned. "And I've been responsible for my fair share of death, lately." The reminder made my stomach turn.

"You're fighting a greater battle. One for good, not evil. And you've only killed those who fight on the side of destruction."

I smiled weakly, but it made me feel a bit better. It still boggled my mind that I was sitting here with my mother after being alone for so long. I'd watched Cass and Del discover their pasts and wished so desperately to discover my own.

Now that I had, I was so lucky I couldn't fathom it.

"Here." My mother handed over the two small boxes. "For you."

The first one, about the size of a cigarette pack and made of wood, contained a lock of hair, carefully laid out. Magic shimmered over it. Something to preserve it, if I had to guess. "This belonged to Ademius."

My mother nodded. "Yes. He was one of the founders of this kingdom, so long ago."

"I will find him." Determination burned within me. "If Drakon has drunk the potion and understands the dragon prophecy as we believe, that means he's found Ademius."

"Perhaps."

"Unless Ademius gave the potion recipe to someone else, he was in Drakon's grasp. Or he's escaped it, in which case he is likely hiding. Either way, he'll be hard to get to."

"It will be difficult, but you can do it."

Her words warmed me. "Could you tell me a bit about him?" I'd need that info to help my dragon sense latch on.

"According to legend, he was tricky and wise. Not a seer, but he had a sense for things to come. That may have been why he left Elesius. A plague came not long after his departure. Perhaps he knew it was coming."

I closed my fist around the box, calling upon my dragon sense. After a while, it tugged at me. "He's in the American west. The desert."

"You've found him, then?"

"It will take time. It's a vague sense of location now, but as we get closer, it will hone in on him."

"Don't go until tomorrow morning. You must rest."

She was right. A short sleep would regenerate my power after the battle and leave me fully prepped for what was to come. I tucked the box containing Ademius's hair, which was kinda gross to think about, into my pocket. Then I opened the next box, which revealed a slender silver bracelet.

"It's a powerful concealment charm," my mother said. "Wear it, and hopefully it will keep Drakon's men from finding you."

I'd once worn one of these to protect myself from the Monster who'd stolen me as a child. But if this one was enchanted to conceal me from Drakon, that could be useful.

"I can't guarantee that it will work," my mother said. "He's amazingly strong if his men have the magic to break through our barrier. But wear it for me. Please."

"Of course." I slipped it onto my wrist. The wide band that Ares had gotten me sat higher on my arm.

"Be careful when you seek Ademius. And we'll be here if you need us."

I hugged her, so grateful to have my mother back. For so long, I'd only had Cass and Del. But now, with my parents and Ares, my world had grown so much larger. My throat tightened and I squeezed my mother's hand.

As much as I wanted to be with her always, I couldn't stay here. Not with my life and responsibilities in the outside world. Cass and Del were my family too. But hopefully I could visit. At least occasionally.

~

I found Ares in his room down the hall. At my knock, he pulled open the door.

"Uh, hi." My gaze went straight to his bare chest. It wasn't that I was a horndog. But I kinda was, because he looked *good.* I jerked my eyes up to his face. "You want to take a walk?"

The corner of his mouth kicked up, and I stared way too hard at his full lips. "Sure."

"Great, I'll uh—just wait here." *Smooth, Nix, real smooth.*

He left the door open and found the towel on the bed, then scrubbed it over his wet hair. He must have just gotten out of the shower. My eyes traced his muscles like he was a sculpture. He dropped the towel. And because I'm super smooth, I blushed and looked away so fast you'd have thought I was spying on his income taxes.

Whistling, I walked down the hall a ways, willing my cheeks to cool. The door shut behind me.

I turned. He wore a dark T-shirt and a smile. Though the smile should have made him look less deadly, I was pretty sure nothing did that. It didn't help that he had a burn on his cheekbone. It just made him look rakish and more dangerous.

"Where to?" he asked.

"Not sure. I just want to explore."

"Fair enough."

We didn't speak as we walked down the stairs and out the door. I was ridiculously grateful that we didn't see my parents on the way out. I wasn't a teenager and he wasn't taking me to the movies or the prom, but it would still feel kind of like that if I saw my parents. I didn't know how to *do* those things. I'd forgotten what life with family was like. Del and Cass were definitely family, but not this kind. Though they might have heckled me before a few dates.

The moon was high overhead, half full and gleaming with

light that shined on the city around us. Golden lanterns hung from buildings and the water fountains made the loveliest noise.

"You're from a nice place, Nix."

"Yeah. Weird, but nice." I turned left, heading up toward the mountains. The street inclined in this direction, but I always liked to get the hard part done first.

Ares walked at my side. It was warm enough here that I'd been able to forego my jacket, and the bracelet he'd given me wrapped around my bicep. I pointed to it. "What is this thing, exactly?"

"Protective charm. Unfortunately, it can't repel shots of magic, but it'll blast anyone who touches you with ill intent."

"Cool, thanks. It saved me from that mage."

"You saved yourself from that mage. It just helped."

I smiled at him. "It definitely did. Where'd you get it? Is it what you went to the Vampire realm for?"

"It was." He raised a hand to the burn on his cheek, as if checking it. It was nothing but a faded mark now. "It's from the Pūķis."

"Really?" I loved the idea that my fiery dragon friends had helped me out.

"Yes. It is imbued with their magic. I'd once heard that they could enchant objects like that, but had never actually seen one." He shrugged. "But with Drakon after you, I wanted you to have extra protection."

"So you went to the Pūķis." We'd reached the top of the street, where there was an open expanse to our left—a dead garden, I was afraid—and a path into the mountains on the right. I chose the path on the right. It almost felt like I could feel a hint of life in the forest around me.

"Yes. Except they didn't understand what I was asking for at first. Hence, this." He pointed to the burn on his cheek. "But eventually they understood what I wanted and that it was for you. It's damned hard to talk to a dragon, though."

"Thanks for trying." I reached out and squeezed his hand. He squeezed back, and we walked like that for a moment.

I released his hand to climb up a rock. The path was becoming windier and more narrow. I could imagine this place with flowers and grass and trees. Devastation made a wasteland of my chest. "All of this is dead because of me."

"Not because of you. *For* you."

"Feels like the same thing."

"It doesn't matter. You didn't want it, you didn't ask for it." His voice was firm, as if he wanted to force me to agree. "And you'll risk your life for whatever fated task you must accomplish. It's your sacrifice too, Nix."

He was right that I'd give it back in a heartbeat if I could. But I was part of something bigger—something I barely understood and definitely didn't feel worthy of.

Up ahead, a glitter of water caught my eye. I hurried forward, the sound of a crashing waterfall delightful in the stillness of the night. Somehow, the water sparkled brighter under the light of the moon, a tall, thin spire of water that poured from the cliff above. I went right up to the edge of it, then turned and surveyed the town below.

It was beautiful, a series of ancient buildings climbing up the valley ridge, the golden lamps like stars spread across the night sky. "It's beautiful."

"It is," Ares said. "It's your home."

"It doesn't quite feel like it, though I'm glad to be here." The word *home* would always be reserved for Magic's Bend. I turned back to the waterfall. Cool mist sprinkled my face. There was space behind it. A walkway. "Let's check this out."

The waterfall fell into a gleaming pool, but there was a ledge that was just wide enough to sneak behind the falls. I started on the path, then looked back at Ares. "Can you do your hand light thing?"

He held up his palm and light glowed from it. I grinned and

turned back, edging into a cavern behind the falls. It was about the size of my apartment. The light from Ares's palm gleamed on the glittering topaz rocks studded into the cave walls. They were the most beautiful gems, shimmering with a deep richness that made me think worlds could be found within them.

"This place is amazing." Wonder filled Ares's voice.

"It is." I turned, awed, to face the waterfall. It still glittered in the moonlight, creating a sparkling veil that shielded us from the world.

Suddenly, I realized how close Ares was standing. He was right at my side, his shoulder just inches from mine. All I could hear was the pounding water. All I could smell was his winter fresh scent. All I could feel was the heat of him.

As if in a trance, I turned toward him. His gaze was hot on mine, his head tilted down because he was so much taller. The light from his hands blinked out, as if he were distracted. By me.

My eyes adjusted quickly, but there were only shadows here. Somehow, it made it easier to feel him, even though we stood inches apart. Tension thrummed in the air between us. My breath caught in my throat.

All I could think of was kissing him—pressing my lips to his and tasting him.

So I did it, standing on my toes and wrapping my arms around his neck. He groaned low in his throat, as if he'd been waiting for this, waiting for permission, and yanked me toward him. His touch enveloped me, his whole body burning against mine when I pressed full length against him.

I could feel the curves and planes of his muscles, the heat of his skin beneath his clothes. Every inch of me lit up. His lips were warm and soft, skilled in their pursuit of my surrender.

A small noise escaped me as I parted my lips beneath his, letting his tongue plunder my mouth. Warmth flowed through every inch of me, a current that made me tingle.

Ares's arms tightened around my waist as he lifted me onto my tiptoes.

"You taste so damned good," he muttered against my lips. "I want to taste you everywhere."

The words stole my breath, images flaring in my mind. Images of Ares and me, doing everything I'd ever wanted to do. Even some things I'd never imagined before now.

His lips trailed from my lips across my cheek, grazing my earlobe.

"You're so beautiful," he rasped.

"I don't need the words." I stared blindly at the ceiling as sensation flowed over me.

"You're getting them." His lips trailed down my neck, his kiss delicate.

When his tongue traced my skin, it flooded me with heat and pleasure. I shuddered. His teeth grazed me, at first blunt, and then sharper.

Fangs.

I should have been terrified, but instead, heat shot through my veins. *Bite me.*

I wanted it more than I'd ever wanted anything. Wanted to feel him inside me.

His tongue swiped out, a lash of electric pleasure between the points of his fangs. All thoughts blanked out of my head. I clutched him to me, nothing but sensation and want and need. I'd have done anything at that moment.

But he pulled away, panting and shuddering.

My eyes flashed open. He thrust me away from him, but didn't let go of my waist, no doubt so I wouldn't fall. Because I would fall. My legs were made of Jell-O.

"What's wrong?" My breath heaved.

Ares's eyes were wide, his fangs white in the dark. "Too close. I was—too close."

"To biting me?"

"Yes." His voice was hard, disappointment clear in his voice.

"But that's not so bad, right?" Vampire bites—as long as they didn't drain you dry—were supposed to be awesome. Especially in situations like this.

"No. No, but… it's a big step. You should think about it. Or at least say yes while you're in your right mind."

Amusement peeked through the desire that was still turning my brain to mush. "You mean, when I'm not under the spell of your sexual charms."

"That's exactly what I mean." He all but growled the words, as if this situation pained him. Which it did, if he was feeling anything like I was. He had to be suffering a real serious case of blue balls right now. In the dim light of the cavern, I could barely make out the tension in his neck and the way his jaw clenched. Yet his hands were so gentle on my waist.

He just wanted to make sure he had my consent before he chomped into me. And frankly, it was awesome.

"Have you learned anything else about the connection we feel because I've had your blood?" I asked.

"I've asked scholars in the Vampire realm, but they know nothing. It's how I found you, though. I was able to track you."

"Wow." I stepped back slightly, stunned. That was kinda huge. But then, I'd felt like I'd sensed him yesterday when he'd arrived at Ancient Magic.

"Exactly. It's strange, but welcome."

Welcome?

Maybe we were fated or something.

Nah. Crazy talk.

"Want to head back?" I asked, desperate to distract myself from any stupid thoughts of being fated with Ares. That was a dangerous path, and one I would not tread.

He stroked my cheek, as if reluctant to leave. "Sure. Let's go."

Ares took my hand, and we left the cave, heading back out into the dying wonderland that was my home.

CHAPTER SEVEN

The next morning, Moira and my parents walked us to the portal where we would leave Elesius. The town was quiet this early, the trickling water of the fountains a soundtrack as we walked down the street.

"This is the same portal that we use when we go on trade expeditions," my mother said. "It will take you wherever you envision on earth."

"Trade expeditions made necessary because I've sucked all the life out of this place."

"No. You did not. Elesius *gave* you its power. You are the chosen one. It is different."

I swallowed hard, hoping I was up to the task.

The portal was at the base of the city, near a massive fountain that spewed clear, cool water. My mother stood in front of me and took my hands. "Be careful, Phoenix."

"Careful is my middle name." Okay, that was kind of a lie.

A small smile curled my mother's lips. "Somehow I doubt that. But we will be here. Now that you have found your way home, you may return whenever you wish. Just think of this place and a portal will appear."

Joy warmed my chest. The idea that I could come back when-ever—that I could have dinner with my parents—was surreal. I hugged her. "I love you."

"I love you." She squeezed me hard and let go.

I hugged my dad next, my heart overjoyed. My parents turned to Ares to say goodbye, and Moira came to stand next to me.

Her voice was fierce as she whispered, "You *must* return. You must stay."

"What? Why?"

"You must."

I frowned, about to ask for more detail, but my mother and father turned back to us. Moira snapped her mouth closed and smiled at them, as if nothing had happened.

"Ready?" Ares asked.

"Yeah." I glanced at Moira one last time. Her insistence made me nervous. I'd get to the bottom of her weirdness, but it wasn't a priority right now. "Let's go."

I said one last goodbye to my parents, then stepped up to the portal. I looked at Ares. "To Death Valley Junction?"

It was the closest town to where my dragon sense said Ademius would be, and we wanted to get started right away. Even better, it was a supernatural town like my own.

"To Death Valley Junction." He reached for my hand.

I took it and clutched the box to my chest with my other hand, then we stepped through, together.

Once again, the world swirled around me, crazy sights and sounds from all over the globe. When I stepped out into the real world, the silence was deafening.

This time, I merely stumbled instead of landing on my face. When my eyes adjusted, I realized that we were in an old desert town. It looked like the Wild West, with a wide flat street made of dirt and wooden buildings running down either side.

There were actual *saloons.*

A freaking tumbleweed bounced across the road.

I turned to Ares and tipped an imaginary hat. "Howdy, Pardner."

He grinned.

"Seriously, though," I said. "I think John Wayne is going to come out of one of these buildings any second. We could duel."

"You'd win."

I punched him lightly on the shoulder. "Thanks."

The dry heat was oppressive, but not unbearable. There were some people walking down the street, going in and out of shops or houses. There were no obvious threats, like angry demons or a corrupt sheriff looking to run us out of town, but still…

"Let's duck out of sight," I said. "I'd like to call Cass and Nix."

Ares nodded. We walked to an alley between two buildings—the Death's Door Saloon and the Murderous Mercantile—and I pressed my fingertips to my comms charm to ignite its magic. "Cass? Del?"

"Nix!" Two voices squawked out of my comms charm, fear and anger obvious in their tones.

"Where the hell have you been?" jumbled over top of "Why the heck haven't you called us?"

"Sorry, guys! Sorry!" Shit. I really should have found a way to contact them when my comms charm hadn't worked in Elesius.

"Where are you? We're coming there right now," Cass said.

"We're in Death Valley Junction, in the alley between the Death's Door Saloon and the Murderous Mercantile."

They said nothing, but a moment later, Cass and Del appeared in the middle of the street, Cass having used her transportation magic to zap them here in an instant. They spun in a circle, their gazes finally landing on the saloon, then hurried toward us.

Del was still in her polar bear pajamas, and Cass's hair was wet. They threw their arms around me.

"We were so worried!" Cass cried.

"Why the hell didn't you call us?" Del demanded.

They stepped back, brows scrunched and gazes angry. I told

them about Elesius—how I'd been so shocked and amazed that I'd been a jerk and forgotten to try harder to get in touch.

"Your family's alive?" Tears glinted in Cass's eyes and her voice rang with joy. "That's so amazing."

"I'm so happy for you!" Del threw her arms around me. Cass joined in.

Tears pricked my eyes as I hugged them back. I was *so lucky*. I'd waited the longest to find my family, but I'd found them *alive*. I pulled back from them. "How are things back in Magic's Bend? Have you learned anything new about Drakon?"

Cass nodded. "Roarke finally had some luck with a contact in the Order of the Magic, though it took him a little while."

The Order was secretive. As the governing body of all Magica —magic users who weren't shifters or fae or vampire—they took their jobs seriously and didn't hand out information easily. Roarke, who worked alongside them as Warden of the Underworld, was the only one among our number who even had a shot at getting info.

"What'd he learn?"

"Drakon's compound on the outskirts of Magic's Bend was bought by a company that paid cash. But their origin is unknown. When they tried to track it, they found nothing."

I sighed. "Not a surprise, considering that he's supposed to be a criminal mastermind."

"But Roarke did learn more from his contacts in the Underworld. Apparently there's been a call put out for more mercenaries. A lot of cash for anyone who joins up. He doesn't know who's hiring, but we bet it's him. And he's hiring hundreds."

Hundreds.

Damn.

Anyone who wanted hired muscle usually went for demons. It was both costly and illegal, but they were strong and had no morals. In order to hire a demon mercenary, you had to perform some pretty complex magic to get them out of hell and onto earth. This guy had that much magic and money? Bad news.

He was building an army and already had the prophecy untangled. Two steps ahead of us.

"Why are we here, anyway?" Cass asked.

"My ancestor was the one who made the vessel of truth. My mother gave me a lock of his hair so that I could use my dragon sense to find him, and this is where it took me."

"Wow, so this has been fated for a long time," Del said.

I nodded. "Seems like."

"So you'll find him and get the recipe for the potion." Cass grinned. "Hot damn!"

"Yeah. Or he's still in Drakon's clutches." I frowned. "In which case we're heading straight for him."

I wished I knew what we were walking into.

"You said this is Death Valley Junction?" Cass asked.

"Yeah."

"There's only one thing this place is really known for," Cass said. "It's the starting off point to reach Hider's Haven."

"What is that?" Ares asked.

"It's where you go if you don't want to be found," Cass said. "Like, *really* don't want to be found."

"It can't be that hidden if you know how to get there," I said.

"I don't, really. Aidan just told me about it. It's supposed to be insanely difficult to get to, and this is just the starting off point. You'll need someone to take you across Death Valley."

"Death Valley?" Damn. If I was supposed to be Life in the Triumvirate, that was the last place I wanted to go.

"Can we not transport across?" Ares asked.

"No. Death Valley's magic prevents it, and that's part of the appeal of Hider's Haven. You have to go through—and mostly likely die—to reach it."

"It makes sense that he's hiding out then," Ares said. "He must have escaped Drakon somehow and doesn't want to be re-caught."

Excitement thrummed in my chest. "Which means we can kill two birds with one stone—learn the prophecy and find out where Drakon is."

"Exactly." Cass grinned.

"We'll come with you," Del said.

"No." I shook my head. "We only need a couple people to find him. And fates forbid that we fail."

"You'll need to pick up the job if we do," Ares said.

"We'll watch your backs as we cross the valley," Del said. "You need us."

"No." I made my voice firm. "You know as well as I do that hunting someone who doesn't want to be found is best done in small numbers. We don't need to scare him. Ares and I can take care of ourselves." I removed the strap that held the box to me and handed the box over to Cass. "And you need to keep this safe, back at our place."

The last thing I needed to do was carry the beaker through Death Valley. That was crazy.

Cass took the box, but opened her mouth as if she were about to argue.

I held up a hand. "This is my fight, Cass. And right now, this is the best way."

She snapped her mouth shut. As worried as she and Del were, they knew I was right.

"Fine, but call us if you need us," Del said. "We can be there in a heartbeat."

"Exactly." I smiled. "So no need to worry!"

She laughed. "Hardly. But be careful."

"And find someone to take you across the valley," Cass said. "You'll need a guide."

"Will do." I hugged her and Del.

We said our goodbyes, and they disappeared back to Magic's Bend, the beaker in tow.

"Glad to have that off my hands." I looked at Ares. "What do you say we head into a bar and try to find a guide?"

"Lead on."

We headed out onto the old street and went into the Death's Door Saloon. We stepped through the swinging doors and I felt like I was in a John Wayne movie. It smelled of beer and cigar smoke. My eyes adjusted to the dim light within.

Though it was fairly early, there were a few men and women at the bar—all dressed kinda like old Western cowboys—and a few more playing pool. I pointed to an old guy with a big white mustache who sat at the end of the bar. "How about him?"

"Why him?" Ares asked.

"Because old guys have done it all and when they're finished, they sit at the bar, knowing it all."

"Good enough logic for me."

I walked toward the bar, choosing a seat one down from my target. Ares sat on my other side. The bartender, a tall man with straight black hair and piercing eyes, came over. "What'll it be?"

"Coffee, thanks." It was too early for beer or whiskey. Not that I'd tell that to the old guy next to me. I pointed to him. "And another one for him. Whatever he's having."

The old man's keen blue eyes raised to meet mine. "Thank ya' kindly. But what's that for?"

The bartender busied himself with the order, along with Ares's coffee, and I turned to the man and smiled. "Hoping you could help us with some information."

His bushy white eyebrow rose. "Information, ey?"

"We're trying to get across Death Valley. To Hider's Haven."

His brows lowered. "Whatcha want to go there for?"

My mind raced. Better to be the hunted than the hunter, if I wanted help. I lowered my voice. "I'm looking to lay low for a while."

The guy nodded at Ares. "What about him?"

"Him too."

"Must be someone bad then."

"Isn't it always?" I accepted my drink from the bartender and handed him a few bills, then turned to the man. "So, do you know anyone who could guide us across the valley?"

"First, it's through the valley, not across." He sipped the whiskey I'd bought him.

I held up a hand. "My mistake. Through the valley."

"Now that we've got that straight, yeah. I know a gal. My nieces lead people through. But it'll cost ya."

"That's all right. Where can we find them?"

"Down at the end of the road toward the west, turn right and look for the house with the buggy out front."

"The buggy?"

He frowned. "Did I stutter?"

"No, I just…" I nodded. "Okay. Look for the house with the buggy out front."

"Yeah. Got a pink ribbon tied on the back."

"Thank you."

He nodded and sipped the whiskey. "Be careful now. The valley ain't no place for the timid."

I grinned. Timidity wasn't my problem. "You have a good day."

I got up, met Ares's eye, and we left. The day had warmed up in the time we'd been in the bar. It might be winter, but Death Valley cooled for no season. I found the rising sun and headed down the street in the opposite direction. We passed a crossroads and a vehicle parked on the dirt side-street caught my eye. I pulled to a dead stop, staring. "Whoa."

"What?" Ares turned to look.

The car was actually a tricked out beast of a machine, painted gunmetal gray, with massive wheels, spikes all over the hood, and the headlights contained in cages. There was another one just beyond it, a similar style but customized differently.

I glanced at Ares. "So I guess they've traded up from horse and buggies."

"An understatement."

We continued down the street, reaching the end and taking a right. There were only a few houses in this part of town, and one had a massive tricked out gray hummer sitting next to two similar machines. The tires were almost as big as I was. They made the one we'd seen earlier look like kid cars. A pink ribbon fluttered off the back of the biggest, meanest one.

"That's the buggy?" I asked.

"Looks like." Ares chuckled.

The body almost looked like an old-school Hummer, boxy and big, but the top had been sawed off to make a convertible. Except that a platform had been erected high over the front seats, big enough for a person to stand on while holding onto a rail that had been fixed to the front. The driver could sit in the seat underneath. There was a similar platform off the back as well. Spikes protruded from the sides, as if it would repel any monster that tried to ram it.

A girl walked out of the house. She was tall and thin, with bleached hair styled in a mohawk. She wore brown leather from head to toe, but it was more apocalypse-chic than anything else. Her tank top was a strappy thing that looked like she'd made it herself, along with leather fingerless gloves and metal bands around her forearms. Black eye makeup streaked around her eyes.

I looked at her, then at the awesomely crazy car. "Holy fates, we're in *Mad Max*."

Ares chuckled low in his throat.

"Need something?" The girl's voice was rough, her posture so clearly saying *Don't fuck with me.*

I approached, realizing as I got closer that she was only

sixteen or seventeen. Another girl walked out of the house. Her hair was black, but otherwise, she had the same aesthetic.

"Who are they?" she asked the blonde.

"Don't know."

The girls looked tough, almost feral, ready to fight or curse at the least provocation. Frankly, they reminded me of Cass, Del, and I at their age, living on the edge and just trying to make it.

"We're looking for a ride across Death Valley." I nodded at the buggy with the pink ribbon. "That yours?"

"Yeah." The blonde watched me with steady eyes.

"I like it."

"Me too." She propped a hand on her hip. "But no can do on the valley."

"We're desperate." My voice reflected that. "Your uncle said you could take us."

"Sure, normally. But the third member of our team is out sick. Wouldn't be the quality of ride we like to guarantee."

I glanced at the "buggy". It was bad ass, but… "What kind of quality ride?"

"The kind where you get there alive." She grinned, but it was more a baring of teeth.

Well that didn't sound good. Not that I had a lot of choice. "We really need to get across. If you can help us out, I'll pay double."

Interest glinted in her eyes. "What are you?"

"Conjurer." And a whole lot more. I pointed to Ares. "Vampire."

"Can you fight?"

"Yeah."

"Got weapons?"

"I can conjure anything. He's got a shadow sword."

"Willing to risk your life?"

"Every day."

She grinned, and this time the smile was real. "Then we're in for a good time. I'm Ana"—she hiked a thumb at her friend—"this is Bree."

Bree approached, dark hair gleaming in the sun. "That'll be twenty grand."

I nearly swallowed my tongue. "For real?"

"We just told you that you might die on the crossing. Which means *we* might die. So yeah, it's expensive. Especially when you're paying double. And it's one way only."

"No returns at all?"

"Nope."

"Okay." We'd just have to figure it out when it was time to leave. "I don't have any cash on me though."

"No problem. I'll give you my bank details, transfer it online."

These girls knew what they were doing. And I had the money, though barely. Our shop paid well. Really well, considering the value of the magic we sold. But I was always funneling the money straight into my trove, so it was rare I had cash in the bank.

At least I was covered this time. I pulled out my phone, finding the signal to be unexpectedly good, and she rattled off some numbers. I made the transfer, then looked up.

"Ready to go?" Bree asked. "If we leave now, we can make it to the crater by early evening. Should give you enough time to make it across before dark and for us to get home."

"We need to get to Hider's Haven, not the crater," Ares said.

"Crater is as far as anyone can take you. After that, you gotta cross on your own," Bree said.

Damn. "Crater it is, then."

"Give us ten," Ana said. "You can sit in the back."

They disappeared into the house and we climbed up into the vehicle. It was a good four feet off the ground, so I had to use the tire to haul myself up into the buggy. It really should have been called The Beast, but I liked the incongruity of "buggy".

"This thing is awesome." I climbed all over, checking out the construction of the platforms and the sturdy bars that held them lofted over the driver. The spikes on the side panels looked like they were coated in something thick and black. Poison.

"With this as our ride, Death Valley deserves its name," I said.

"It's an impressive machine." Ares looked at me, eyes sharp. "You like cars?"

"Yeah." I almost said *Duh*, but then realized he hadn't been in my trove. "But yeah, I do."

"Careful!" Ana shouted. "That Ravener poison will kill you in a second."

I turned to see her striding out of the house, a bag hanging from her hand. Her sister strode along at her side, heavy boots thudding on the sand. Climbing harnesses were wrapped around their legs and waists. Aviator goggles were propped on their heads. They looked like bad-asses—skinny, teenage bad-asses whose eyes were too old for their age. But I'd been the same once.

They climbed up into the buggy, Ana taking the wheel and Bree sitting next to her. Ana cranked the key in the ignition and the engine roared to life, a throaty growl that would have given my Challenger Hellcat Fabio a hard-on.

She peeled out of the town, heading for the mountains in the distance, then shouted back over her shoulder. "Bree will take the front platform. One of you on the back when I say so."

"What's coming at us?" I shouted.

"Anything! The valley changes what it throws at us." I caught sight of her grin in the rearview mirror. "The humans call it Death Valley because of the heat. Little do they know."

Bree laughed. "We're headed off the main track. Away from the tourists taking pictures. There's a parallel valley—the *real* Death Valley—that only supernaturals can access."

"They say it's where the magic of hell seeps up from the ground," Ana shouted as she stepped on the gas. The buggy flew across the desert, the huge tires eating up the ground. The mountains looming in the distance grew nearer and the heat more intense.

When Ana reached the first valley, mountains rose up on the left and right.

"This is the main valley," Bree shouted.

She pulled a right, speeding over the scrubby ground toward the first row of mountains. She drove straight for one of the shallower inclines—which was still pretty danged steep—and the buggy climbed onto the mountain, tires digging in. She was a pro, weaving around boulders or steeper bits until we crested the ridge and got our first good look at the real Death Valley.

CHAPTER EIGHT

A long valley stretched out in front of us. It had to be at least a hundred miles long and several miles wide. The ground swirled in different colors and seemed to shimmer with heat. An aura of danger hung over the place, dark magic that made my hair stand on end.

"Welcome to hell!" Ana cried.

"She sounds happy about it," Ares muttered.

I grinned. These girls were nuts, but I could relate. Cass, Del, and I had mellowed a bit, but not that much.

The buggy ate up the ground as it sped toward the valley floor. Once we hit the bottom, Bree tossed a harness into the back seat. "Back platform person, put that on!"

Ares grabbed it, shoving his legs through the straps.

"Hey!" I shouted.

He buckled the thing around his waist and grinned wryly at me. "I'm sure you'll have your chance to kick some ass."

"I'd better." I'd see to it.

"Hook the harness to the bar on your platform in case you get knocked off the vehicle—the heat of the sand can kill you if you lay on it too long." Bree pointed to the red button on the front of the harness. "Hit that if you need to release the harness quickly."

"Got it." Ares climbed up onto the back platform as Ana drove like a bat out of hell across the flat, arid land. He latched his harness to the bar.

"I recommend kneeling on one knee," Bree shouted as she climbed onto the front platform and hooked her harness on. Her black hair whipped in the wind. "If you end up on the ground, keep running. Don't stand still on the hot ground."

The sky was a cloudless blue as the buggy raced across the plains. The mountains rose high on either side of us. Ahead, the ground almost appeared white.

"Badwater coming up!" Ana shouted.

The buggy hurtled toward the white surface. It looked a heck of a lot like the Rann of Kutch, the salt plains I'd gone to in India last week.

Until a massive crystal of salt speared out of the earth, right in front of the buggy. Ana dodged it by an inch, driving like a pro, but another one speared out of the ground in front of us. There was no time to dodge without the buggy rolling.

My heart leapt into my throat. We were screwed.

Magic swelled on the air as Bree threw out her hands. A massive sonic boom hurtled toward the salt spear, blasting it to pieces. Ana drove straight through the rubble, laughing.

But the spears continued to surge out of the ground. Ana dodged what she could. Bree blasted the rest, avoiding a collision that would crush the front of the buggy.

They were an amazing team, but eventually, more spears started to pop up in front of us. More than Ana could dodge or Bree could blast.

My mind raced, trying to figure out what I could conjure. I hadn't yet learned to throw my destroyer power in front of me, and it was too slow for this.

Ares slammed his hand against the red button on his harness

and leapt from the buggy, hitting the ground running. He sprinted ahead of the buggy, his vampire speed in full effect.

My breath caught in my throat. I'd never seen him go so fast. This was Ares unleashed. He hurtled toward the salt pillars in the distance, slamming into them with enough force to blast them apart. They crumbled beneath the brute force.

Bree whooped a war cry at the sight, sending sonic booms at the other pillars, smashing them to bits. Ana dodged the rest, weaving the buggy through the spears of salt like this was a deadly game of Frogger.

Ana and Bree were a hell of a team.

Finally, the salt flats ended. Ana drove by a sprinting Ares, who leapt up and grabbed the rail on the back of the buggy, swinging onto the back platform. Sweat dripped down his face and he was panting, his chest heaving like he'd run a marathon in ten minutes. Which he kind of had.

"Not bad, vampire!" Bree shouted. "Now clip on your harness!"

"Safety first!" Ana cackled as she hit the gas and plowed forward.

We really were in Mad Max—Bree just needed a guitar that shot flames. Though I had a feeling she'd use it as a weapon before making music with it.

Ahead of us, stone arches loomed in the distance. We hurtled toward them, the buggy eating up ground. Ana drove under the first one, which was easily forty feet tall.

"Get ready!" she shouted.

The ground ahead of us heaved upward, a massive figure growing up from the dirt. It was shaped like a man, but it was made of gravel and at least twenty feet tall. It grabbed up a scoop of earth, which was really just a giant rock, and hurled it at us.

Bree blasted it out of the sky with her sonic boom, but the next one was aimed for Ares. In a flash, he conjured his shadow sword. His magic flared, the scent of a cold winter morning at odds with the heat all around us. His shadow sword pulsed with the power, and when it collided with the rock, the stone exploded in a blast of powder.

Ana drove through the arches, trying to dodge the rocks that the giant hurled. As we neared the beast made of gravel and sand, Bree shot her sonic boom at a slender spear of rock that protruded right over the monster's head. It plummeted from its perch, crashing onto him. The gravel that created him crumbled to the ground.

Bree whooped.

But another monster appeared farther in the distance, as large as the first. It hurled more rocks, right at us.

Bree blasted them out of the air.

Ares cut them down with his sword.

I felt spectacularly useless.

Until one of the rocks glanced off Bree's shoulder, throwing her back into the buggy. Her harness kept her from flying out, but she dangled limply in the passenger seat.

I hit the red button on her harness, allowing her to collapse into the seat, and leapt upon the platform. We were nearly to the monster, but without Bree's power to blast a rock onto his head, we were in a pickle.

We were nearly to him, a hundred meters away. I had only a second to think.

The arch above his head caught my eye. In a flash, I conjured a bow and an arrow that had a grappling hook end. A long rope trailed from the back of the arrow.

I aimed for the arch, firing. The arrow flew straight and true, sinking into the arch above the monster's head. I grabbed the rope, leaping off the platform and swinging through the air.

Behind me, Ares roared. I swung for the giant's head, realizing suddenly how insane this plan was. I neared him, hoisting myself up onto the rope and praying that he was a conglomeration of loose gravel and not a solid rock monster.

Man, I'd be so screwed if he was one big rock.

I swung for him, feet first, my boots colliding with his head. He crumbled, collapsing through the ground. Victory soared through me, quickly replaced by panic. I was swinging straight for the solid rock wall. An image of the Wile E. Coyote smashing into a cliff while chasing the Road Runner flashed in my head.

An insane laugh welled within me, but I managed to twist myself just enough to plant my feet on the wall and push off, swinging for the buggy as it sped by. I released the rope and landed in the back seat, an awkward pile of shaking limbs and trembling muscles.

"You're insane!" Ares pulled me up, his gaze frantic with worry.

"You ever need a job, you call us!" Ana cackled, speeding out of the arches and away from the threat of gravel monsters and flying boulders.

Death Valley was insane.

Panting, I climbed up so that I was standing on the back seat, my butt propped against Ares's platform. Ana was leaned over the seat, looking at me and shaking her head. "Stone cold."

"Thanks." I searched the terrain ahead of her. "There's sand dunes up ahead."

"The Guantlet," Bree said. "Haven't seen that one in a while."

"The obstacles change frequently?" I asked.

"Depending on the season, or the valley's mood, yeah." Ana slowed the buggy to a stop before the sand dunes and Bree leapt out, crouching by one of the tires.

"What's she doing?" I asked.

"Letting out some air," Ana said. "Better for sand driving."

Bree raced around the buggy, finishing the job, then jumped back into the passenger's seat. Ana took off.

Bree ducked below the seat, looking for something. She popped up again and tossed two pairs of steampunk-looking goggles back at us. "Put those on."

I tugged them on, the world suddenly going strangely reddish. "The color will help you see the snakes."

"Snakes?"

Bree shot me a grin as she tugged hers down. "Yeah. Big ones. Better get those swords ready."

Ana looked at Bree. "Ready to take the wheel?"

"Yeah." Ana took Bree's place—all without slowing the vehicle.

Ana climbed onto the front platform, then looked back at us. "Get ready for some heat. And swords at the ready."

"It's always summer in the gauntlet." Bree laid her foot on the gas, speeding toward the golden, rolling sand dunes.

I called upon my magic, conjuring a long blade. But if there were going to be snakes... I conjured a shield as well, handing it to Ares. Then I conjured another.

As soon as the buggy passed over onto the sand, it slowed slightly, the tires plowing over the golden stuff.

Suddenly, the heat was intense, a pounding fire that beat down upon my head. Sweat rolled down my face. I'd been in deserts before, even magically enchanted ones, but this was incredible.

Rain began to fall from the sky, sizzling when it hit the hood of the buggy. A drop hit me, burning like fire. I yelped.

Acid rain. Made of actual acid.

Ana knelt on the platform, raising her hands to the sky. Her magic swelled, bringing with it the scent of rain, and it shined from her hands, forming a barrier over us like a dome. The magic was gray and opaque, some kind of surreal mist that blocked the sun and acid rain.

I had no idea what her gift was, but it was working. The heat lowered to a bearable level. But Ana looked like she was about to collapse, the effort making sweat pour down her face and her muscles tremble—as if she were Atlas, holding up the world.

"Ana's got the heat under control," Bree yelled. "But it's all you now! Goggles on!"

A moment later, sand whirled up to form a tornado around us. It pinged against my goggles, blurring my vision even more. But through the whirlwind, I caught sight of a slender green whip of a thing.

Snake!

It darted toward me, fangs white enough to shine. I thrust my shield up, swinging out with my sword. The blade sliced through the neck of the beast. The head dropped to the ground.

From the back platform, Ares took out one of his own. Ahead, Ana kept the blazing sun off us. The wide back seat made a pretty good platform for fighting sand snakes, which popped up every few meters, striking for the vehicle. Some collided with the spikes, shriveling and dying within moments. But those with better aim, I took care of.

One struck straight for Bree, fast as lighting. I lunged for it, slicing it through the body as her hand whipped out and grabbed it around the neck, squeezing it tight. She kept her other hand on the wheel.

I laughed, amazed at her sheer badassery. She was only a teenager.

She chucked the snake to the dirt and put her hand back on the wheel, driving us over the sand dunes like a pro while her partner held the weight of the sun on her shoulders.

Finally, after we'd slain countless snakes and Ana looked like she was about to pass out, we exited the sand dunes. The sandstorm died and the valley opened up in front of us. Ana dropped her shield and the sunlight returned, the heat dissipating and the horrible acid rain disappearing. Immediately, Ana collapsed into the front seat, panting.

"Not bad!" Bree shouted.

I stood on the seat, surveying the terrain that we'd driven into. The mountains still loomed on either side and the desert stretched out in front of us. Scrub brush grew low on the grounding patches, eking out a living in this tough terrain.

"You guys been doing this long?" I shouted.

"Three years." Ana dug some water out of the footwell of the buggy and tossed us bottles. "It suits our magic, which can be a little out of control sometimes."

"Doesn't matter in the valley," Bree said.

She had a point. Cass had once had a lot of trouble controlling her magic. This would have been a good place for her. Out here, there was nothing but sand and monsters to witness your wildness.

Bree stopped the buggy and jumped out, a steel tank of compressed air under her arm. She refilled the tires, then climbed back in and cranked on the engine. It roared to life and we zoomed off.

Wind whipped my hair as we drove through the valley, having a brief reprieve from the challenges. We passed a ghost town in the distance. The sight of the empty ramshackle buildings sent a shiver down my spine. What had happened to those people?

Bree slowed the buggy and called out, "Almost there!"

Eventually, she pulled to a stop beside a large crater. It at least half a mile across, with sides that sloped down to a flat bottom hundreds of feet below. Though it appeared empty, dark magic welled up from the bowl, making me shiver.

"This is where we leave you," Ana said. "Good luck."

"Any tips?" I asked.

She grinned. "Don't die."

"And Hider's Haven is a bit farther along," Bree said. "Won't be easy to get to, especially if you don't have an invitation."

Shoot, we definitely didn't have one of those. Not that we could worry about it now. I climbed down out of the buggy, followed by Ares. The girls looked down at us from their seats.

"Thanks for the ride," I said. "You sure you'll make it back across okay?"

They grinned. Bree said, "We've got some aces up our sleeves. We'll be fine."

"Really?"

"The desert takes a rest at dusk," Ana said. "Only quiet time of the day. It's why we schedule our journeys like this. Gives us a chance to get back safely. You were just lucky you showed up when you did or we'd have had to wait till tomorrow to cross."

"Be sure to get across the crater before dark, though," Bree said.

The sun was hovering just over the horizon, shedding an orange glow over the desert. It was gorgeous, but in a threatening way, because it didn't give us long.

"Can't we go around?" I asked.

"No can do." Ana shook her head. "Gotta earn your way into Hider's Haven, and crossing the crater is part of that. If you cheat, the next phase of the journey won't be revealed to you."

Damn. Sometimes magic was a pain in the butt.

"And I suggest camping out overnight once you reach the other side," Bree said. "Just take a snooze and wait for daylight."

"Yeah." Ana grimaced. "Don't want to meet the creatures that go bump in the night here."

"Thanks," I said.

They waved goodbye, then peeled away, tires kicking up dust. I hoped they made it back safe. As for us, we'd just have to figure it out.

I turned, surveying the terrain. The crater was deep—at least four hundred feet down—but the sides were sloped enough that we wouldn't have to rappel. To my left, there was a sign with a picture of a falling man and the words *Don't Fall In.*

Ha.

I looked at Ares. "Ready?"

"As I'll ever be."

"I guess the plan is simple. Fight whatever comes at us."

He grinned. "Works for me."

Man, this was so different than working at my shop. There, I was in control. The unexpected happened—but it was always the same variety of unexpected. Demons breaking in, thieves trying to get away with our hard work. I knew how to take care of that.

But this… this was all different kinds of unexpected. And that's where the trouble was.

I saluted Ares and stepped off the ledge, skidding along the slope down into the crater. The gravel was loose under foot, and a breeze blew my hair back as I slid down. I felt a huge grin stretch across my face. I was sliding into danger, but this part was fun.

Ares and I reached the bottom at the same time. It was darker in the pit, shadows cast by the setting sun.

"Warmer here," Ares said.

"Yeah. Feels like the crater trapped the heat." The other side was probably about half a mile away. A shame we couldn't transport across. Even if it wasn't impossible, it violated the *earn your way in* rule. That meant crossing the crater.

I bent down and picked up a rock, then hurled it into the middle of the crater. It landed about fifty meters away. Not the worst throw. Thankfully, it didn't sink into the ground. "No quicksand there. You try."

Ares picked up a rock and hurled it. His bounced to the ground about a hundred meters in the distance. He picked up another and threw it farther. It, too, bounced.

"Good enough for me." I stretched, meeting his gaze. "Ready to run?"

"Let's do it."

"Go faster than me if you need to. I can take care of myself."

"Sure."

"Ha. Liar." It was in his eyes. He wouldn't leave me.

"Don't worry about it." He took off, sprinting ahead of me.

I followed, close at his heels. As expected, he didn't race ahead of me.

At first, it was fine. The heat sent sweat rolling down my spine and my breath came hard as I sprinted. We made it halfway across before the air turned cold, an icy chill that smelled of snow and felt like a dark winter night. A bit like Ares's magical signature, but not.

It was more than normal cold, and fear shivered over me, raising the hair on my arms.

Ahead of us, the air shimmered, coalescing into the forms of men and women. They glowed a transparent blue.

Oh, hell. "Phantoms."

CHAPTER NINE

Most were dressed in old-timey wear, like the hapless souls who'd crossed this desert in carriages in the nineteenth century, looking for a better life. They hadn't found it. They'd died here.

"They'll go for your worst memories or fears." I panted. "Try to close off your mind."

Easier said than done. There was no fighting Phantoms with blade or bow. Only Del could do that, because she was half Phantom. I was about to press my fingertips to my comms charms and call her when the Phantoms surged forward.

They were fast. And hungry.

Within a second, they were nearly upon us, their soulless eyes devouring us. I felt the cold tendrils of their magic inside my mind, reaching for my darkest memories and dredging fear to the surface.

Too late to call Del.

I sprinted forward, trying to avoid them. We just had to get past them before their influence drove us to our knees with misery and pain.

But that was the hard part. Their dark magic seeped inside my mind, tendrils of dark mist that pulled at memories of my time in the Monster's dungeon. Of being all alone in the dark and the cold. Once again, I was fourteen, huddled against the wall of my cell.

Then an image of my *deirfiúr*, killed by Drakon. Their bodies, lifeless in the dirt.

A sob burst from my chest, but I pushed myself faster, running past Phantoms who tore at my mind with their magic. They reached for us, flowing toward us as we passed their haunting grounds. I dodged around them.

A glance at Ares showed his face twisted with pain. What was he reliving?

There were more Phantoms ahead, and we were only a quarter of the way through the crater. My muscles weakened as I ran, as if the strain on my mind were too much for my body.

"Failure," one of the Phantoms hissed.

"Unworthy," hissed another.

They'd found other fears to go for. I could feel their glee at my pain, a dark magic that pulsed on the air.

I sprinted harder, but somehow only managed to run slower. They were too strong, too fierce. And we were only halfway across.

We wouldn't make it.

"Go!" I cried to Ares. He was fast enough.

But he stuck by my side, actually veering closer. Like he was considering picking me up or something. But that wouldn't work. He'd still be too slow.

We wouldn't make it across. *He* wouldn't make it across. Images of him being devoured by the Phantoms' dark magic streaked through my mind. I couldn't bear it.

I stumbled, going to my knees. He dragged me up, though he didn't look much stronger than I was. The strain was too much. The misery overwhelming.

Desperate, I called upon my new destroyer magic. I'd never successfully thrown it before, and it wouldn't work against Phantoms, but I had to try. There was nothing left to do but try. I gathered it inside myself, then hurled it outward at the Phantom who reached for me.

A blast of gray smoke collided with him and he stumbled back. Victory and hope lightened my heart, lending strength to my muscles.

Until he surged forward, stronger than ever. He glowed brighter, his magic battering my mind. Pain surged through my skull, a migraine that would lay me out if I weren't so driven by adrenaline and fear.

The Phantom had *liked* the destruction power. Of course he had.

And why was I throwing that at him, anyway? I was *Life.* It was such a weird power to have.

I shouldn't be using that. It was counter to my very being.

Instinctually, I called upon the magic at the core of my being. Not a magical gift, like conjuring or destroying, but the power that actually fueled those gifts. The power that lived within my soul. It was raw magical energy, the battery that fueled my magic. I'd never used it this way before—I didn't know that it was even possible—but fear could make a person try crazy things.

The magic was a golden light inside my chest, fierce and strong. I let it free, calling it up from inside myself until it filled me with warmth and hope. I sprinted through the Phantoms who stood between me and the other side, stumbling only once.

I gathered up the magic like it was spun gold, then threw out my hands and hurled it at the nearest Phantom.

Golden light shot from my palm, colliding with the monster. He shriveled to nothing in an instant, blinking out of existence like he'd never been.

Shock stole my breath—though that could have been all the sprinting—and I tried it again, this time aiming for a group of Phantoms coming for Ares.

The golden light flashed, hurtling from my palm and colliding with the oncoming enemy. They blinked out of existence, the magic too much for them.

We had a chance!

We were still fifty meters away from the other side of the crater. I was beyond exhausted, and there were at least a dozen Phantoms between us and safety.

But I had a weapon.

"On your left!" Ares shouted.

I threw a blast of golden light at the Phantoms. It was smaller this time, but it collided with two of them and obliterated their glowing blue forms. We dodged the next group, my legs straining and my lungs aching. Though they ran to keep up with us, we were just fast enough.

There was one last group between us and the other side. Five Phantoms, all with their arms outstretched and their gazes hungry. There'd be no dodging this many—not when they stood directly in front of us.

I gathered up the last of my magic, every single bit of it, and hurled it at them. Golden light burst from my palms, flashing toward them. It bowled the Phantoms over, destroying them in seconds.

Joy surged in my chest as exhaustion dragged at my legs. But we made it to the edge and began to claw our way upward. My lungs burned and my muscles ached. I scrambled toward the top on hands and knees. Ares wasn't doing much better, the mental strain of the Phantoms was enough to give even him trouble.

We reached the rim and I scrambled up, flopping onto my back and panting as sweat rolled down my face. It was warmer up here, the unnatural chill of the Phantoms long gone. I rolled over and peered into the crater below.

It was empty, as barren as when we'd first looked into it. Though we'd left some Phantoms behind, they'd disappeared as soon as we had left.

"Well done, Nix." Ares panted, rising to sit at the edge.

I dragged myself up into a sitting position, scooting toward him. The sun had sunk fully behind the horizon and the dark was creeping in on us.

"What kind of magic was that?" he asked.

"I have no idea." But I felt empty inside, totally exhausted. "I think it was my core magic. I just threw it out of me. I didn't even know I could do something like that."

"You blasted them with life."

"Maybe?" It sounded crazy, but… "I guess it makes sense. If the plants on Elesius all died to give me their magic, that's what it would be, right?"

"I think so." He reached for my hand, squeezing. "You saved us back there. Phantoms… I've only ever heard of them. They're worse than I ever realized they could be."

I shuddered at the memory of the horrible fears they'd dredged up, the awful things they'd made me relive. "They're the worst. Something so terrible that you can't even fight."

"But *you* can fight them."

"I guess I can. Now." I smiled. That was a good power to have. Except for the fact that I was tapped out. I could feel the slightest tingle of magic inside me. My power had started to regenerate, a battery recharging, but it'd take more rest.

And now was truly the worst time to have no magic. It was dark, the air was growing colder, and I was thirsty. Soon, I'd be hungry. "I'm pretty tapped out. Won't be able to conjure water or a tent for a while."

Ares started to rise. "I'll go look for water."

"No." I reached up and grabbed his hand, pulling him down. "Remember what Bree and Ana said? We need to hang tight when it gets dark. Who knows what's out there?"

"My vision is good. I'd see them coming."

"All the same, I don't think we should separate." I tugged his arm again, and he sat. "I'll be able to conjure some simple things soon. Then we'll camp out till morning."

He sighed, then sat. "All right."

He tugged me closer, wrapping an arm around my shoulders. His warmth flowed into me, seeping into my tired muscles. I sagged against him.

"How's your hearing?" I asked. "Extra good, right?"

"I'll be able to hear any approaching threats, if that's what you're asking."

"That's what I'm asking." I leaned my head against his shoulder, enjoying the closeness. "Though I do trust Bree and Ana. If they said to camp here, it's safe."

"Mostly."

I laughed, but he was right. You never could quite tell what would come at you. And those girls were so brave that their idea of safe could still be pretty dangerous.

The night grew darker as I rested against Ares. Wind whistled and the air grew cooler. Stars came out, glittering high in the sky above. Eventually, I had enough power to conjure us some water and sandwiches, along with a big sleeping bag.

"You're impressively resourceful," Ares said.

"Conjuring is a good skill to have." I polished off my sandwich and took a sip of water, then huddled into the sleeping bag.

Ares joined me, and I curled up against him, seeking his heat. The desert was cold at night, down to the forties at this hour. Though being close to him set my blood on fire, I was too exhausted to sit upright, much less do anything else.

"Not just the conjuring," Ares said. "You created new magic today. You saved us from the Phantoms."

I sighed. "Yeah. A bit of a surprise."

"Really?"

"Yeah. The new magic was a shock. And... I've been doubting myself a lot lately."

It felt good just to say the words out loud. Even feeling doubt could be guilt inducing. Like I should be strong enough not to feel uncertain in the first place. Which was just a vicious circle.

But saying it out loud... kinda took the burden off.

"You're one of the strongest, most resourceful people I know." Ares's arm tightened around me.

"It's just that I only have the conjuring power. It's super handy. But if you're up against a seriously powerful magic, conjuring a sword doesn't get you very far."

"It's gotten you pretty damned far, I think."

I smiled. "I'm proud of that. I am. But one day, I'm going to be out-powered."

"That's a risk for anyone. But fate wouldn't choose you if you weren't worthy."

"Thank you." And maybe he had a point. I'd blasted those Phantoms away with my new magic. Magic from Elesius, which had chosen me over all my ancestors. "Considering everything that my city had given me, I really ought to have had some faith. To honor its sacrifice."

"Doubt can be a tremendous burden. It will slow you down."

I looked up at him. Moonlight cut across his face. "You know something about that?"

"I do. For a long time, I thought I couldn't uphold my father's legacy as Enforcer. Or be worthy of the post at all."

"But you are."

He shrugged. "Took some time to realize that. But I'd have been better off if I'd have realized it sooner."

"How did you realize it?"

"Just forced myself to do the job and give it my best. Eventually, I started to believe in myself."

"Not a bad plan." It was something I needed to do. Just try— try to succeed, try to believe I could do this.

Yeah, there was a lot at stake. And sometimes I felt like I was standing at the base of Mount Everest in flip-flops.

But getting mired in doubt was a terrible way to spend the magic that Elesius had given me. I owed it to myself to have a little faith in my abilities. I owed it to my home.

"You're going to be fine, Nix. I've always believed in you. And I don't say that easily."

I smiled. Whatever came my way, I'd do everything in my power to stop Drakon. To finish what fate had started for me.

"Thanks." I snuggled closer to him, exhaustion dragging at my muscles. It was pretty awesome to confide in Ares. Scary, to get this close to another person, but awesome. Really freaking awesome.

～

I ran through the forest, leaping over tree limbs and dodging boulders. Tears poured down my cheeks, fear turning my chest to ice.

All around me, the forest died. Trees lost their leaves and grass shriveled to nothing. Elesius was dying, but Mum wouldn't tell me why. She said I was too young to know, but I was thirteen! Nearly an adult.

I scrubbed the tears from my cheeks, but my blurred vision made it impossible to see the tree root. I tripped, sprawling on my hands, pain shooting through my knee. A rock.

I sobbed, head bent.

The forest was betraying me. As if it were my fault it was dying. I shook my head.

"No," I whispered. That was crazy.

I rolled onto my butt, sitting with my back against the dead tree that had tripped me. All around, wind whistled past the trees. But there were no leaves to rattle. No grass to wave in the wind.

At my side, there was a tiny, struggling vine. It leaned toward me, as if blown by the wind. But the wind came from the other direction. I reached out to pet it.

A footstep sounded behind me.

I whirled, catching sight of the old man who occasionally visited me when I was in the forest.

"Grandfather Ademius!" I called. I sniffled, shoving back the tears.

He turned his head in my direction and smiled, as if he'd been looking for me. I hadn't seen him in ages.

"Where have you been?" I asked. Happiness fluttered in my chest.

He approached slowly. He said he was slow because of his old bones, but there was something timeless about him.

"Well?" I prodded.

"Calm down, child." He smiled, but it didn't reach his eyes. "It's harder for old Ademius to get around these days."

"You could just come live here, you know."

He tutted. "That I could not. And I have my reasons." He held up a finger to still my usual arguments. "But it doesn't mean I can't visit you."

I smiled, leaning back against the tree. He sat down to join me, his joints creaking. Ademius had started appearing to me years ago, but only while I was in the forest. I thought of him almost as a woodland sprite, though he wasn't very spritely at his age. He'd said he was my family, one who'd had to leave Elesius long ago. He looked a lot like my mother, especially around the eyes, so it was clearly true.

I loved his company. Though I had my parents, my grandparents had died before I was born. Ademius was the closest thing I had to a grandfather.

"Have you done your gardening today?" he asked.

"Yes." He always asked about my garden, giving me tips and tricks. "But I'm worried. Not only has the forest been dying faster, now my garden is starting to look wilted. The herbs are failing. That's never happened before."

Ademius's eyes turned sad, but he nodded knowingly. "It was only a matter of time."

"What do you mean?"

"Things can't live forever, child." He gripped his walking stick. "Not even me."

Mention of his death distracted me from my worry over the forest. "You've lived a long time, but why not longer?"

He smiled. "I've lived plenty long. You have no idea. But don't you worry about me. It's you we have to talk about."

"Me?"

"Yes." His gaze met mine, suddenly serious. "I will have to go away soon and won't be able to visit you as often."

"You only come a few times a year, at most." I dug my hands into the dirt. I couldn't lose Ademius.

"Be that as it may, I must leave." His eyes were kind. "But you will find me again, one day."

"How?" Tears pricked my eyes. This felt final.

"You'll know the way. It will be inside you. But I have left something for you that will help. When the time comes, your mother will give it to you."

"Like a map?" This was like a game—except it was sad. What was the point of a sad game?

"Like a map, yes. But it's inside of you." He held out a hand, silencing me. "While I'm gone, you must take care of your garden. Learn to tend it."

"Why is that so important to you?" I loved my garden, but I almost thought he loved it more.

"It is important to you, Phoenix. You must tend to the life within your garden. It will reward you tenfold."

"Okay." That was weird. What did he even mean by that? "Do you really have to leave now?"

He nodded, then slowly rose, leaning heavily on his cane. I jumped to my feet, throwing my arms around his frail body. I sniffled, but the tears wouldn't stay back any longer.

"I can't believe you're leaving," I sobbed.

"I must. Someone is hunting for me. Someone evil. I must not fall into his hands or..." I drew in a shuddering breath. "Just tend to your garden, Phoenix. It will love you in return."

≈

I popped awake, gasping. The sun peaked over the horizon, spreading a golden glow over the valley.

"What's wrong?" Ares's voice was groggy as he sat up.

"A dream." I scrubbed my hand over my face to dry the tears. "I knew Ademius when I was a child."

Suddenly, things were falling into place.

"How?"

"He visited me in the forest several times a year. He must have known what I would become. But then he disappeared. He said he was being hunted."

"By Drakon?"

"I think so. He said he was evil."

"That means Drakon has been seeking this prophecy for over a decade. He didn't have the Vessel of Truth at that point, though, did he?"

"No. He first got it by stealing it from us. But that doesn't mean he didn't know the legend of the beaker. Vessels of Truth are rare. He could have learned of Ademius first, then found the beaker."

"And Ademius got wind that he was coming for him and ran for it," Ares said.

"Exactly. But not before telling me to tend to my garden." I smiled. Though I couldn't remember the other times I'd seen him in the forest, I could recall how comforted I'd felt to be in his presence. How much I'd enjoyed talking about my garden with him. "I've always liked older people and I wondered if I had a grandparent. I didn't—not technically. But I'd had Ademius."

"He's a grandparent." The corner of Ares's mouth quirked up. "If you add about one hundred 'greats' in front of his name."

I smiled, my heart suddenly light. We were going to find Ademius. More family for me.

I climbed out of the sleeping bag and stretched my sore muscles. "Come on. We've got to get a move on."

"Excited?" he asked.

"Yeah." I gazed out at the rising sun, hope filling my chest. "Last week, I knew nothing about my family. Not even if they were alive or dead. Nothing. I've been desperate to know for ten years. But now, I have parents. And Ademius."

"That is a good streak of luck." Ares smiled.

"Yep. And I'm going to keep it going." I called upon my magic, conjuring a breakfast of cheese sandwiches and water. I handed one off to Ares.

"Cheese sandwiches for breakfast?" he asked.

"Cheese for all meals."

"Thanks." He bit in. Chewed. Swallowed. "You're a good cook."

"Only with the conjuring. And cheese." I ate my sandwich quickly, then conjured a simple nylon backpack. I crouched down and bundled the sleeping bag up into a tiny packet. I'd been careful to conjure one of those compressible ones. I hated leaving trash behind, so I'd just carry it out of here, along with our used water bottles.

"You don't want to use your destroyer power to clean up?" Ares asked.

"No." I shoved the sleeping bag into the backpack. The destroyer magic felt too dark inside me, more so than ever. Was that because I was becoming more in tune with the Life magic and the two couldn't coexist easily? Though it was controlled and no longer making me ill, I didn't like using it. "I don't want to use it more than necessary. And I should save my power anyway."

"Fair enough." Ares reached for the backpack and swung it onto his back.

"I don't mind carrying it."

"It feels like a feather on my back. Literally."

"All right, Superman."

Ares grinned. "Just a vampire. But I'll take the title if you insist."

I laughed and punched him playfully on the shoulder. "Lets get a move on."

We set off across the desert, following my dragon sense toward the mountains in the distance. The sun blazed down, making me wish that Ana and Bree had been able to stick around with their buggy. Too bad I couldn't conjure a car. I was getting close—all that practice with fixing up Fabio and his siblings was giving me enough of an understanding of a car's inner workings that I should be there soon.

But for now, we were on foot. The ground was too uneven for a bike, so we were stuck with walking for at least two hours. In the blazing sun.

Yuck.

As the hours passed, the sun grew hotter and hotter. Finally, I spotted something.

"I think we're almost there." I pointed ahead of us, to the mountain that loomed in the distance. There was a massive rock at the base, like a huge flat boulder that had rolled down the mountain and settled at the bottom.

When we neared, it became clear that the rock had been placed there intentionally to block something. An entrance, probably. Hider's Haven was in there. Or through there. Hard to say.

I eyed the massive rock in front of us. It had to weigh several tons, no question. "Well, that's not going to be fun."

"We have to move it to get to the path beyond?" Ares asked.

"Yep." I inspected it. Magic shimmered around the stone, a haze of white that indicated a spell could remove it. "There must be some kind of password to get by."

"Perhaps that's what Ana and Bree meant when they said it would be difficult to get in without an invitation."

"Makes sense." I examined every inch of the stone, then started checking the mountain around it, looking for some kind of clue. When I helped Cass and Del on their jobs, we sometimes had to figure out riddles to get through the tricky parts of tombs and temples. Usually, I was pretty good at them.

But this time? "I've got no idea how to get through."

"I'll try to move it."

"It weighs thousands of pounds."

"True." Ares approached, eyeing the slab of stone. I could almost see the calculations going on behind his eyes. He rubbed his hands together, then crouched at the edge of the rock and gripped a small crevice. He heaved upward.

Ares strained, veins standing out at his neck as he grimaced. The rock shifted, scraping against the mountain. It lifted a centimeter off the ground. Two centimeters.

Sweat rolled down Ares's temple. His face turned red. He grunted. The stone lifted another few centimeters, then dropped to the ground.

Ares cursed and stepped back. "Too big."

Hmmm. That left me then.

I probably couldn't destroy the whole thing with my magic—this was about a thousand times bigger than the dishrag I'd obliterated in practice a couple weeks ago. But I had to try.

I called upon my magic, stepping forward and pressing my hand against the stone. I shuddered, not wanting to call upon the destroyer magic, but forcing myself to. It felt weird, especially once the power rushed up inside me, but I focused on pouring the magic into the stone. It rushed out of me as a breeze, filling the rock.

Slowly the stone cracked, a fissure crawling from the top to the bottom of the enormous rock. The slab didn't crumble away—I wasn't strong enough for that—but the crack grew slowly.

I focused, feeding more of my power into the stone, envisioning it splitting in two. Finally, the crack crawled all the way up to the top. It was now in two pieces. Hopefully I could destroy at least one.

Panting, I stepped back. "Just give me a moment and I can try again."

"Not necessary." Ares stepped up and gripped the rock on the right, heaving it upward. His muscles strained, but the boulder crept up inches. Then a foot. He shifted it a few feet away from the mountain, then dropped it. It thudded to the ground. He stepped back, sweat trickling down his brow.

"Nice one." I held up a hand for a high five.

Ares grinned and held up his hand so that I could smack it with my own.

"Good teamwork," Ares said.

"We should make our own motivational poster. I'll be the kitten hanging off the branch and you can be the eagle who is soaring toward his goal."

Ares chuckled.

I joined him at the crevice where the stone stood away from the mountain and peeked inside. It was dark and narrow, but there was a darker bit and the cool scent of earth flowing out.

"Definitely a tunnel back there, and just enough room to squeeze through." I was about to step inside when Ares slipped past me and went first.

He had to exhale fully and slide through sideways, but he managed to disappear into the tunnel entrance. I shuddered at the close quarters, then followed him.

Inside, Ares held his hands up, letting his magic light shine inside the dark space. It was about seven feet tall and ten feet wide, a railroad track disappearing down the tunnel.

"It's an old mine," Ares said.

I crouched, examining the track and the footprints in the dirt. "The track hasn't been used in decades, but the footprints look fresh. Sorta."

"Hider's Haven could be a repurposed mine."

"I'd almost bet on it." I stood and started down the track. Ares kept at my side, his hands illuminating the passage in front of us.

The air was dark and cool down here. For the first time since the sun had come up, I wasn't sweating. "Hider's Haven has got to be in this mountain. It's not a throughway."

"Between the heat and the monsters out in the valley, I agree."

I kept my ears pricked and my senses alert as we went deeper into the mountain. Soon, a pale glow shined from up ahead. I pointed. Ares nodded.

We crept toward it on silent feet. As we neared, the glow coalesced to form a figure.

"A ghost."

"Not a Phantom?" Ares asked. There was a slight shudder to his voice. I couldn't blame him.

"No. Phantoms are blue. This guy is just a ghost." They didn't normally give the living too much trouble. This one was transparent white, about forty years old, with long messy hair covered by a hat. His overalls and old-time hat making him look like he'd stepped out of another century. "A miner."

We neared, and I waved awkwardly. "Hi."

He chewed on something, his jaw working furiously, but I couldn't tell what he was chomping on. Then he tipped his hat. "Howdy. You got your pass?"

"Um." I tensed, ready for a fight. "No."

He frowned. "Hmm. Then I reckon you ought to turn back."

"Can't do that." Ares stepped forward.

The ghost seemed to debate, then shrugged. "Can't stop ya. But you'll regret it."

"Going farther?" I asked.

He grinned, revealing several missing teeth. "Yep. But it gets boring down here, so I wouldn't mind the company."

"We won't be here long," I said.

His smile widened. "You will be. Once the mine gets ya."

"Because we don't have a pass?" Ares asked.

The miner nodded and hiked a thumb behind him. "You won't make it two hundred yards. But give it a try."

"You're quite the welcoming committee," I said.

"Like I said, I'm bored. Heard that boulder crack and came to see what's up." He waggled his brows at me and licked his lips. "And you're real pretty."

"Ew. Haven't you ever heard of subtle charm?" He'd really lost me at the lip licking. *Blech.*

"You'll change your tune once you're stuck with me for a century." He smacked his lips.

"I'm quite confident that I won't."

"Well, we'll see. No one's ever made it through who don't have a pass."

And now they were ghosts haunting this place. Probably avoiding the creepy advances of the lip-licking miner.

"Then where are the other ghosts?" Ares asked.

"You'll meet 'em." He cackled. "And then you'll be one of 'em."

"Great. Thanks." I left him, Ares at my side.

"Come and find me later!" the miner hollered after us. "I'll be lookin' for ya!"

"Ew, no," I muttered and continued on. The path felt like it could go for miles, the railroad running deep into the mines. We'd walked for ten minutes or more, the tunnel dark and quiet. Eventually, a ghost hovered along the side of the path ahead of us. "Fingers crossed for a non-sleazy ghost."

Ares chuckled. As we neared the second welcoming committee, I got a good look at him. My stomach dropped. Half of his head was crushed in.

"Looks like he fell from a great height," Ares said.

I swallowed hard. "Yeah."

We were close enough to see his ghostly brains and sightless eyes. Though we passed him, his head didn't turn to look at us. A shudder ran over me. Apparently the brain injury had wounded even his ghostly brain.

We were a few feet away when one horrible whisper slid across the back of my neck. "*Run.*"

Fear poured ice water over my skin.

I'd never been more convinced in my life that I should do as I was told. The one word was desperate, terrified.

I glanced at Ares, heart in my throat, then took off, sprinting down the corridor. Running toward our doom.

CHAPTER TEN

The ground trembled beneath my feet, creaking and groaning. I sprinted harder, racing through the tunnel with Ares at my side. We followed the train tracks deeper into the mine.

The ground in front of me dropped away, a huge section disappearing into the depths of the earth. I lunged left, avoiding the deep crevasse. Another section of ground dropped away.

I leapt onto the wooden slats of the train tracks. It was like a suspension bridge across the disappearing ground. I leapt from wooden slat to wooden slat. Some crazy part of my brain reminded me that they were called ties. Not really useful info at this point, but apparently I was crazy.

"Faster!" Ares shouted from behind me.

All around us, sections of ground dropped away. The train track remained, the wooden ties held together by the iron rails. I leapt from tie to tie as the earth fell away around me.

Suddenly, what had happened to the ghost was obvious. He had fallen, his skull crushing against the ground far below.

Shit. That would be us.

As the ground fell away, the train track bridge became too

long. My heart thundered. The track wasn't built for this—it was going to snap. And we were going to fall.

I inanely wished for a jet pack, but it was beyond my conjuring capabilities. So I called upon my magic, ready to create another bow and an arrow with a grappling hook end. It'd worked once, so I just prayed it would work again.

But the bridge snapped. All thoughts of conjuring fled as I fell. My stomach jumped into my throat as I reached out for the wooden railway ties. My fingertips slid off the rough wooden surface of one tie, but I managed to grip the next as the train track bent toward the newly formed cliff wall like the broken rope bridge from Indiana Jones.

I'd always thought that scene was insane. Now I was living it.

The cliff wall in front of us was jagged, with little ridges where one could stand.

"The metal will snap!" Ares roared from below me.

I glanced down. He clung to the ties below me as we swung through the air. Above us, the iron railroad ties were bending as the bridge drooped.

"You'll have to jump for the cliff!" Ares shouted.

We were close enough that I just might manage to grab onto one of the little ledges.

The metal shrieked as the train track bent too far. I scrambled to find footing on one of the railroad ties beneath me. As soon as I did, I pushed off and jumped for the cliff.

As I sailed through the air, it hit me how impossible this was. Even in the movies, people didn't succeed at this. Ares flew by me, strong enough and fast enough that he defied reality.

I reached out, stretching for the little cliff. My fingertips brushed the stone surface, but didn't find purchase. My throat closed with terror.

Until Ares's hand wrapped around my wrist, jerking me to a stop.

I panted, dangling above the endless drop. Ares dragged me

up. I scrambled onto the shallow ledge, clinging to the rock in front of me. To my left, the train track snapped and plummeted into the darkness below.

Sweat ran down my back as I pressed my face against the cliff wall. "Thanks."

"No problem." Ares panted, his back pressed against the cliff.

The ledge that we stood upon was only a couple feet wide. I looked up. The main part of the tunnel path was about twenty feet above us. Fortunately, there were little ledges like this one that we could use to ascend.

"If we're careful, we can climb up," Ares said.

I nodded, my muscles shaking as adrenaline poured through my veins. "That was insane."

"We got lucky that the tracks didn't snap sooner."

"And that you've got crazy vampire strength and speed." I'd have gone splat without him. Why was it that the desert always lent itself to Wile E. Coyote antics? I drew in a shuddery breath. "Ready to climb?"

"I'll go first."

I followed Ares up the cliffside, clinging to the rock ledges. When we reached the top, I flopped onto my stomach, gasping. I gave myself a few seconds, then sat up and looked back down the tunnel, the way we'd come. A huge portion of the ground was missing, plummeted into the earth. The ghost with the crushed skull stood on the other side, watching us.

I waved.

He didn't wave back. The earth that had fallen away began to knit itself back together, magic putting everything back to rights. Within moments, the ground looked normal, as if it'd never broken apart at all.

"Hider's Haven has some serious protective enchantments." I turned to look at Ares, who was getting to his feet.

"That won't be the worst of it."

I stood, joining him. We set off down the path. I kept my eyes glued to the ground in front of us, heart in my throat. The train track continued, stretching deep into the mountains. I inspected the walls to try to figure out what had been mined here, but I saw no traces of valuable stone or metal. An empty railway car shoved up against the side of the tunnel revealed no goodies either.

"Up ahead." Ares pointed to a ghostly blur ahead of us. It lay along the ground, almost like a puddle.

I hurried toward it, dread in the pit of my stomach. As we neared, I realized that the ghost was a flattened person. And it wasn't cartoonish. I swallowed down bile. "He looks like he's been crushed by a steamroller."

Run. The ghost didn't say it—he couldn't say it—but I heard it in my head all the same.

I took off, sprinting down the corridor with Ares at my side. What the heck could flatten a man like that? Ideas flashed through my mind, each more horrible than the last.

When the mountain began to groan around us, stone scraping against stone, I realized.

The walls had begun to close in on us from either side, an inch every second. Dread chilled my skin. Immediately, I conjured a heavy iron bar on the ground in front of me, hoping that it would slow the mountain from closing in on us.

I leapt over the bar and left it behind, praying it would work. We sprinted as the walls ground toward us. Then they stopped. I glanced behind. The iron bar was straining as it held the walls apart.

"Faster," Ares said.

I sprinted, breath tearing through my lungs. "Leave me."

He was so much faster that he should just race ahead.

A loud *snap* rent the air. The walls rushed in on us. The iron bar had broken. My heart thudded as I conjured another, then another, leaving them on the ground behind us.

The walls stopped their deadly movement. I pushed myself until my lungs burned.

Snap. Snap!

The walls began to close in once more. They were only a foot from us on either side, the corridor now only three feet wide. Ares cut behind me so that I could race ahead, making me want to scream my rage. He'd never save himself if it meant leaving me behind.

It drove me insane.

I conjured more iron bars, but they wouldn't hold the walls forever.

"We're near the end!" Ares shouted.

Up ahead, the corridor widened. I gave it my all, sprinting as the metal bars snapped behind me. The walls closed in.

They were nearly brushing my shoulders by the time I spilled out into the main hall, where the walls didn't move, thank fates.

Ares squeezed out behind me, his broader shoulders scraping against the enclosing stone.

I bent over, panting and sweating. My lungs were on fire.

Ares hadn't even broken a sweat—not since he'd spent the run behind me.

"You really just need to leave me behind sometimes," I gasped.

"You totally had that." He sounded slightly winded, at least. "Good work with the iron bars."

I stood up and scowled at him. He grinned, then leaned forward and kissed me, his lips pressed hard to mine.

I enjoyed it for a half second before pushing him back. "You need to take me seriously, you know. You *should* try to save yourself. Don't risk your life like that."

His gaze turned somber. "It's my life to risk. You can't make that decision for me."

My heart stuttered. He was right. I *couldn't* make those decisions for him, nor should I. But damn it, I didn't want him dying for me. Which he seemed willing to do. It was crazy.

"I knew we'd get through that," he said. "I believed in you."

"Uh huh." I nodded, my heart and brain flopping around like fish out of water. He sure did say the right things. And it really sounded like he meant them. This was all too much for me. So I avoided it and turned. "Let's go."

We started down the path, jogging slowly alongside the railroad tracks. The farther we went into the mountain, the staler the air became. Then it got fresher.

"Air's weird," I muttered.

"We're coming up to something."

In the distance, the walls of the corridor glowed golden and bright. My dragon sense roared, covetousness welling within me. Though my trove was full of plants, cars, and weapons, the dragon side of me was a huge fan of gold. *Huge.*

It liked gold like a cat liked tuna.

The gold tugged at my dragon soul, pulling me down the corridor toward the glowing golden lights. I ran faster. As we neared, a white glow coalesced to form a ghost. Again, he was dressed like a miner. But this time, he was covered in deep cuts that dripped pearly white blood.

I shivered.

The ghostly miner just shook his head at us and whispered, "Go back."

"Not really an option, friend," Ares said.

"I gotta agree with you," I said to Ares. "But given how the last two challenges have gone…" The smart part of me wanted to listen to Mr. Bled-To-Death.

Of course we wouldn't. Couldn't.

Ares reached for my hand and I took it, then walked by the messenger. Sadness tugged at me for all the people who'd lost their lives down here. I shoved it aside and we continued on.

It didn't take long for the golden lights that glowed in the walls to coalesce into slender figures. They were made entirely of gold, with gleaming eyes and six-inch claws on each hand. The way they stepped out of the stone wall was eerie enough to make me shiver.

And to make my dragon sense go wild with joy. It was an idiot sometimes.

"Any idea what these are?" I asked as I warily watched their claws and called upon my conjuring gift.

"Bad news."

There were five. Then six. Seven. More stepped out of the walls. All were at least as tall as Ares, but so slender they looked like reeds.

I let the magic well inside me, letting a crazy idea take form. The monsters' claws were sharp, but gold melted at an extremely low temperature.

I conjured a flaming torch, then a big bottle of hairspray. I passed both off to Ares. "The torch is coated in thermite to burn extra hot. I think you can figure out the hairspray."

Ares grinned and took them both, holding the torch up in front of his face like some bad-ass explorer from old. Firelight danced off his features. I conjured my own torch and hairspray, then eased toward the creatures.

"If they charge—"

As if the beasts understood my words, they did just that, rushing toward us. They raised their claws, which glinted in the light of my flame.

They swiped out, going for blood. I held out the torch and pressed the button on the hairspray. Flame roared, jetting toward the creature, which lunged back. Another monster swiped for my legs, going low and almost making contact. I dodged out of the way and thrust my torch toward him, firing the hairspray. The wild flame collided with his hands, softening the metal of the claws until they dripped gold.

Jackpot.

Ares fought at my side, aiming his hairspray and torch like a pro. I raced ahead, dodging the gleaming golden monsters.

Pain sliced through my calf. A cry escaped me as I stumbled. I forced the agony from my mind and spun, swiping out with my torch and hairspray. The flame collided with the arm of one of my attackers. The creature skittered back.

Ares fought off three golden beasts, his torch streaking through the air and his shield blocking their blows. Fortunately, he was fast, melting their claws before they could make contact.

We fought our way through the crowd, unable to really kill them but at least able to hold them off.

I was sweating and covered in a few deep scratches by the time we made it to the end of the corridor. They stopped at an invisible barrier, clawing toward us but unable to get any farther. They were completely silent, which was eerie. Without mouths, there wasn't much they could say.

I lowered my torch and empty bottle of hairspray. My heart thundered as I watched them try to get to us. Thank fates for the magic that stopped them. They could only haunt the section of tunnel that had been enchanted.

Ares turned to me, his gaze concerned. "Are you all right?"

"Fine." My wounds burned, but I could ignore them. I thought. "Let's get a little farther away."

We left the golden beasts behind and hurried down the corridor. I limped only slightly, which I considered a win. Once we were a few dozen feet away, I sat on the ground and inspected the deep scratches on my calf. They bled sluggishly, but it wasn't the worst I'd ever gotten.

Ares knelt, raising a wrist to his mouth.

I held out a hand. "No. It's not that bad."

Especially since I didn't know what his blood would do to me. We already had a connection and he could find me. Could it get deeper?

Whatever I felt for him… I wanted it to be *my* feelings, not some weird supernatural blood bond.

Instead, I conjured a bandage and wrapped it around the

wound to stem the bleeding. The rest of my cuts were so superficial that they needed no binding, though one of them was ruining my Black Widow T-shirt.

"You okay?" I eyed Ares, searching for any wounds. There were none that I could see.

"I'm fine." He stood, reaching a hand down for me. I took it, letting him haul me up.

"I sure hope that's the last of it." I turned and continued down the corridor.

We went deeper and deeper into the mountain. Eventually, the railroad tracks disappeared. "Do you think we're past the old mining operation?"

"Could be." Ares cocked his head. "Hear that?"

I shook my head, hurrying to see if I could hear it when I was closer. Eventually, the indistinct sound of people—like lots of people chatting in a bar—drifted down the hall. I reached out a hand for Ares, slowing him.

We crept along on silent feet. The sounds grew louder. Definitely a lot of people. Ahead, the tunnel curved. We crept around the corner. Two men sat on bar stools on either side of the tunnel. Behind them, the tunnel opened up to a vastly larger space.

"They look like bouncers," I muttered to Ares.

"Then pretend we belong inside."

Was this really the end of the journey? Had we reached Hider's Haven? My dragon sense tugged hard, confirming it was likely.

I sauntered up to the bouncers like I belonged. They were two big guys, burly with muscle and pale skin that looked like it hadn't seen the light of day in centuries. Probably because it hadn't. Their beards were long and their eyes beady.

"Hey guys," I said.

"Pass?" The one on the left, who I thought of as Bushy Beard Junior, held out his hand.

"I lost it." I smiled, trying for charm, and tilted my body so that they couldn't see the blood staining my shirt.

"Liar." Bushy Bear Senior scowled at me.

"Don't call her a liar." Ares stepped up beside me, shoulders squared.

Okay, it was testosterone time. The two bouncers surged up, chests out and fists up. We weren't getting through them without a tussle.

But Ares was quick. His vampire speed was a blur as he punched them both in the face. Like cartoons, they stood still for the briefest moment, then keeled backward.

I gave him a thumbs-up. "Nice job."

"Better unconscious than dead." He flexed his hand. "No need to kill the guards."

"Couldn't agree more." I knelt and conjured two gags and ropes to bind their limbs. Ares and I made quick work of trussing them up, then we left them propped against the wall and headed toward the entrance to Hider's Haven.

My dragon sense went wild as we neared the archway. Ademius was here somewhere. I could feel it.

Since confidence made a person look like they belonged, I sauntered through the archway like I was the quarterback walking through the doors of the high school.

The space within took my breath away. It was like the central courtyard of a European village. Except that it had been built right into a mountain. The room was large, at least the size of a football field. Vaulted ceilings were streaked with golden ore. Light glittered off the ore, illuminating the space with warmth. Holes in the ceiling had to be vents for fresh air. Magically enchanted to encourage airflow, I'd bet.

All around the courtyard, shops and cafes were built into the mountain. They were small, but impressive all the same. The space was full of people, sitting on benches and at tables, chatting and playing cards. Though Hider's Haven was charming in the extreme, most of the inhabitants had a dubious air about them. The kind that spelled trouble in their past. Which made sense, considering they were hiding out.

But they couldn't be all bad, considering that there was greenery in the courtyard. Several oak trees grew right out of the ground.

"I'd like a gander at that irrigation system," I said. "And the light situation..."

"You like plants?" Ares asked.

"You could say that."

A woman nearby turned, her keen eyes on us. She was about sixty, with a face that said she'd done it all and seen it all and wouldn't put up with any BS. Her magic smelled like an old shoe that a wet ferret had chosen for a house.

"You're not from around here," she said.

"New," I said.

Her green eyes narrowed. "The Council never said anything about that."

Shit. We did not need to be caught as outsiders.

"They should have," I bluffed, heart pounding. "We were invited by my ancestor, Ademius."

She studied me, clearly debating whether or not to buy my story. "Hmm. Then you won't mind if I tell him you are here."

I jumped on it. "Yeah, take us right to him. That'd be perfect."

"If there's one inkling of Ademius not wanting you here, you're going in the pit. Immediately."

"Uh, the pit?" I swallowed hard and looked at Ares. "That sounds bad."

"Oh, it is." She grinned, revealing teeth sharpened into points. Fangs. Suddenly, the charming atmosphere of this place became obvious for what it was—a thin veneer. The people here were hardcore badasses and most likely criminals. "The pit is full of sand vipers. It's where we put intruders. It's perfect, you see, because the vipers will devour the body and leave nothing for us to clean up."

"Whew." I mimed wiping the sweat off of my brow. "Good thing Grandad Ademius is looking forward to seeing us again."

Her eyes flashed with skepticism, but she just turned. "Follow me."

"Laying it on a little thick there, aren't you?" Ares said.

"Maybe." Sweat trickled down my back when Fangs, as I'd started to think of her, waved a hand and several creepy people joined our little party. She was getting backup. To throw us in the pit.

I *really* hoped Ademius would recognize me now that I was an adult.

"If this goes to crap, we're screwed," I whispered to Ares. *Maybe*, just maybe, we could fight our way out of here, but I had my doubts. We almost hadn't made it in. With this lot after us...

Fangs led us through the main courtyard. The magical signatures of the inhabitants battered me from all sides. Dark and light, good and bad. These folks were a mixed bag—some violent criminals, some just hiding from whatever hunted them.

I shuddered, praying that I never ended up in a place like this.

We passed through the courtyard and went down a narrow passage. Doors dotted the way. Some were propped open to reveal small houses, though most were tightly closed.

Fangs stopped in front of one and grinned creepily at us. "The moment of truth."

Considering that there were now about two-dozen makeshift guards surrounding us, things were looking iffy. These folks were serious about protecting their own. Not to mention, they were also probably bored and looking for a scuffle.

I prayed to fate that Ademius would realize who I was.

Fangs knocked on the door. I held my breath. After an endless moment, it creaked open.

An old man peered out, mussed white hair sticking up in all

directions. He looked the same as always, with my mother's eyes and his wooden cane.

A thrill rushed through me to see him again.

"Ademius, there's someone here for you," Fangs said.

Fear widened his eyes and he stiffened.

Shit.

Fangs turned to me, her gaze triumphant. *Into the pit with you.*

"Uh, Great Grandad Ademius?" I said. "I'm Phoenix Knight. I mean, Lividius. Do you remember me? I'm here to see you about something you made long ago."

His gaze darted to me, confusion flaring only briefly before understanding dawned. It was followed by awe. "You're here."

Tears welled in my eyes. "I missed you."

Fangs grunted, clearly disappointed, but I ignored her. She stepped back from the door and I passed by her.

"Don't you step a toe out of line," Fangs said.

I thumbs-upped her, which I didn't think she liked, then stepped into Ademius's small home. Ares followed. Once he was in, I shut the door, grateful to put something between me and Fangs.

I turned to Ademius. Unable to help myself any longer, I threw my arms around him. "I can't believe I'm seeing you again."

He hugged me. "How you've grown."

I pulled back, wiping my eyes. What an embarrassment of riches my family life had turned out to be.

"Welcome," Ademius said.

His home was small but cozy, with stone furniture built into the wall and colorful fabric cushions making it more comfortable. It looked well lived in, like he'd been here since he'd left me in the forest.

"You've learned you are the chosen one," Ademius said.

"So we're getting straight into it?"

"You don't have a lot of time."

"I don't." But I also didn't love hearing the label *Chosen One.* Didn't they always die at the end of the movie?

Ares stepped forward, hand outstretched. "I'm Ares Warhaven."

Ademius shook his hand. "Quite a name."

"I know."

"Come, sit." Ademius gestured us over to a small table pressed against the wall. There were three chairs.

We each took one. I opened my mouth to explain why we were here, but Ademius spoke. "Have you been well these last ten years? Practicing your magic with your garden?"

I smiled at the reminder of how much he'd loved my garden. Now I knew why. "I haven't practiced as much as I should. I lost my memory for a long time. I've just now learned of my plant magic."

Worry creased Ademius's features. "It's more than plant magic."

"I know. I just don't know the extent of it. Do you?"

He shook his head. "I do not. But you must learn. Fast."

"I will."

"So you're here about the Vessel of Truth."

"I am."

He sighed. "I made that so long ago. One of my first tasks as a Wizard."

"It was beautiful."

"It was, yes. Not a Ming Vase or a Faberge Egg, but beautiful in its own way." He drummed his fingers on the table. "That was a different time. A simpler time. I didn't know until later why I felt compelled to make the Vessel of Truth, but I've since learned."

"Because I would need it?"

"Yes. I didn't know that when I visited you. I have the slightest bit of seer blood. Not enough to see the future, but enough to get inklings. I knew only that you were important to me and the future. So I came to see you. And I liked you. I still would, I imagine." He frowned. "If only I'd known then that you would need the Vessel of Truth. It would have saved so much misery."

"Oh no." My stomach dropped. "It was Drakon, wasn't it?"

His gaze darkened, fingers stilling. "It was. The man you fight, Drakon, found me last week. He made it clear what he needed. As soon as I saw you at my door, I realized what you'd come for."

Dread curled in my belly. "Did he hurt you?"

"Enough."

Tears pricked my eyes. I'd failed Ademius. "I'm so sorry."

"Don't worry, dear." Ademius tutted. "I'm thousands of years old. I've experienced worse."

"Whatever it was, it was bad enough to make you give him the recipe for the potion that will ignite the Vessel of Truth."

"All true." He shuddered. "But it is over. I escaped. He didn't have me for long. And you will defeat him. But you must be prepared. His evil… It is incredible. I've never felt anything like it."

I was grateful he didn't go into the details of his time with Drakon. But my soul burned for vengeance.

Ademius stood, retrieving some paper and a pen. "You are here for the recipe, correct?"

"Yes, and to see you. I'm so happy you're still alive. When you disappeared all those years ago, I was devastated."

"I'm sorry dear. It was unavoidable. But you're here now. And I can give you the recipe. In all my years, I've never forgotten it. Complex, but manageable."

Ademius scratched out a list of ingredients, and then a short note that I couldn't read from across the table. He pushed the paper toward me. "I hope you have a skilled potion master for this. One wrong move, and the potion will obliterate the Vessel."

"Yikes."

"That's one way of putting it."

Ares spoke for the first time. "Would you be able to take us to the place where Drakon held you captive?"

"No." Ademius's voice whipped out. "Absolutely not."

My heart tore at the fear in Ademius's voice.

"We need to find him," Ares pressed. "It's the only way to stop him, and you're our only lead."

Ares was right. And I was desperately glad that he was asking this question. I could not have done it.

"I cannot." Ademius shook his head. "I have done my part, the part fated since I was born. I am done now."

"Please." Ares's voice softened, gentler than I'd ever heard it. "Lives are at risk. Thousands of them."

Ademius sighed. "I cannot go back. But I can direct you to a man who can help. He found me while I was trying to escape and helped me."

I jumped at it. "Thank you."

"Don't thank me yet. There is no easy way to access Drakon. But Torus hates him even more than I do. He lives at the edge of Drakon's land. Perhaps he can help you sneak in. Though it won't be easy."

Yeah, it'd probably be a giant pain in the butt. Death Valley style. "That's okay. I'm not expecting easy. I just need a clue. Something to help me find him."

"Then you'll have one." He held out his hand, nodding toward the piece of paper he'd given me that contained the recipe for the potion. I handed it over. He scribbled something on it—a name and a place, it looked like—then handed it back to me. "There. He is a thin man with dark hair and eyes. He loves horses, so I imagine you'll find him at the stable."

"What else can you tell me about Drakon's lair?"

He frowned. "Not much. It is a massive, evil castle. I was kept hooded for most of my time there and did not see much. I only managed to escape when they were taking me to the village to get more supplies for a second batch of the potion. That is where Torus found me. But that is all I know. Godspeed, Phoenix. I always enjoyed our time together."

I reached across the table and squeezed his hand. "We'll tell you when we've defeated them. Then you'll be free to leave here."

"It will not matter. Now that you have the information you need, my part is finished." He sighed, both contented and a bit sad. "I will cross over."

"Cross over?" Dread filled my chest.

His tired gaze met mine. "I'm thousands of years old, Phoenix. I've been waiting for you for a long time. I'm ready for the next phase."

Death. I swallowed hard.

"No. Please don't," I said. This is what he'd meant when he'd said he couldn't help us find Drakon. His time was up. "Please."

Ademius smiled. "I must, child. The magic that made me immortal is linked to you. It allowed me to wait for you. But now that my role is done, the magic will fade."

Tears pricked my eyes. I'd only had him back for a short time. I'd gotten cocky, crowing about all the family I had.

Fate didn't like that.

"Don't be sad for me, Phoenix." Ademius smiled. "I'm happy to go. I want to see old friends and family."

"You will?" I didn't know what happened in the afterlife, but that sounded great. And Ademius sounded so happy about it.

"I will. I don't know everything, but I do know that."

I gave a watery smile. His contentment radiated from him. As much as the idea of his passing tore at my soul, I couldn't help but appreciate that.

"I'll miss you." My voice broke.

"I'll miss you, too. But you'll see me again."

Tears pricked my eyes. His voice was so final. But at peace. I hugged him. He wrapped his arms around me briefly, then stepped back.

"It is time for you to go now," he said.

I nodded, somehow hating the words even though I knew he was right. It was time to go. Time to go and face my fate.

CHAPTER ELEVEN

We were escorted out of Hider's Haven and told never to return. I was okay with that, especially once I stepped out of the tunnel and back into the open air of Death Valley. Even though this place was deadly as a six-headed rattlesnake, at least we were free out here. Out in the open. Not trapped like rats in a sewer, hiding from the daylight.

"I'll miss him." I reached for Ares's hand.

He took it and squeezed. "I know."

A sob tore through my chest. I let it out, then sucked in a breath and held it. I wouldn't cry. Later, maybe. Definitely. But for now, I couldn't mourn Ademius. He'd helped me. In my youth, and now. I had to honor that by succeeding.

I drew in a shuddery breath and turned to Ares. "Okay. I'm good."

Sadness glinted in his eyes. "I'm sorry, Nix."

I smiled, the corners of my mouth trembling. "Thanks. But it's fine. Just getting my parents back was huge. Getting to even see Ademius again was a gift. I need to focus on that. Count my blessings."

"You're one tough FireSoul."

"Thanks." I looked out over the desert. "Now let's get out of here. Could you try to transport us? Maybe it'll work since we're at the edge of the valley."

"I can try."

I crossed my fingers, praying that Ares's transportation ability would work.

Of course, it didn't.

"Damn it," Ares said.

I looked up the mountain. It looked safer than trying to get across the valley. "We need to climb out."

"Lead on."

We began to hike, scrambling up the mountainside. The recipe in my pocket burned. I'd memorized it on the walk out of the tunnel just in case something happened to it. Now, we just had to get home so Connor could whip it up. If anyone could whip it up, it was the gifted potion maker.

Within minutes, sweat dripped down my spine. Though the sun was inching toward the horizon, the late afternoon was still hot as Ares with his shirt off. My muscles ached and my breath came fast as we climbed.

Finally, after what felt like ages, we reached the summit. It was more of a ridge then a point, and we crested it.

"Damn." Ares raked a hand through his hair.

I gazed out at more mountains. We were going to have to go up and down, up and down to reach the edge of the range. "Damn is right."

"Hopefully Death Valley's magic will fade out before the mountains do." Ares started down the other side. I followed, hurrying to keep up.

Halfway down, he reached for my hand. "Let's try again."

It didn't work, but fortunately, one ridge later, it finally did. The ether sucked me in, throwing me through space alongside Ares.

We stumbled out onto the main sidewalk in front of Ancient

Magic. The cool winter air was a shocking change from the heat of Death Valley. The sun was setting behind the trees.

"Holy fates." I shivered. "Let's get out of the cold."

My stomach grumbled as if it agreed.

"And let's get you something to eat," Ares said.

"Ha. You can't say you're not hungry, too." We hadn't eaten since earlier this morning.

As we hurried toward P&P, my dragon sense tugged me back toward my apartment and my trove. A visit sounded really good right about now, but we needed to eat and hand this potion recipe over to Connor.

As we made our way down the sidewalk, I kept my eyes peeled for any of Drakon's minions. Though they couldn't track me because of my mother's bracelet, they knew I lived here.

Across the road, there was a flash of movement. I stiffened, calling upon my magic.

Ares touched my arm. "It's okay."

"There's someone there." I pointed to a large tree. A man leaned against the base, his body braced for battle.

"He's one of mine."

I glanced at Ares, confused. "A vampire?"

"I set several guards along the street. They've orders to wait for Drakon's men to show and take a prisoner if possible."

Though I appreciated the sentiment, I didn't like the secrecy. "You didn't think to mention this to me?"

"To be honest, it slipped my mind. Once you disappeared, that was all I could think about."

I sighed. "Fine. But next time, tell me. That's an important thing for me to know."

"Agreed." He gestured to the man who leaned against the tree.

The guy approached. As he neared, I realized that he was almost as big as Ares. Not many people could claim that.

"Got your best men on the job, huh?" I asked Ares.

"Of course."

The man stopped in front of Ares. "Sir. Nothing to report."

"Not a single demon or any of Drakon's men?" Ares asked.

The man shook his head.

"I wonder if he's distracted?" I said. "Otherwise, wouldn't they wait for us here? He can't track me as long as I wear my mother's bracelet."

"Distracted by what, though?" Ares asked.

"Can't be good for us, whatever it is."

"Definitely not good." Ares turned back to the vampire. "Thank you for the report. You may return to your station."

The vampire gave a sharp nod and turned, walking back to his post. We headed into the warmth of P&P. It was business as usual here, with a small crowd of weeknight regulars and music selected by Connor. The Grateful Dead, tonight. Connor's shirt even matched, the rainbow bear strutting across the black background.

The sight of Connor behind the counter and Claire slinging drinks while dressed in her mercenary wear made warmth fill my chest. Though I was still missing Ademius, it was good to see my friends.

Connor's face brightened when he saw us. "You're back!"

"Safe and sound," I said.

"Did you find what you were looking for?" Claire asked.

"I did." I approached the counter and handed the paper off to Connor. "Do you think you could make that?"

He stared down at it, dark hair flopping over his forehead. "Yeah. It'll take a little time to brew, but I could have it ready by tomorrow morning. Midday at the latest."

"Thank you. You're a hero." My stomach growled loudly.

"Your stomach agrees." Connor grinned. "Cheese quiche with a side of cheese scone?"

I slid onto a barstool, my hunger now clawing at my insides. "Definitely."

"Now you're really a hero," Ares said.

Connor bowed. "I do what I can. You want the same?"

"Yes, thanks."

Connor saluted and headed back into the kitchen. I touched my fingertips to the comms charm at my neck. "Del? Cass?"

"Are you all right?" Cass demanded.

"Fine. I'm fine."

"Whew." Del's voice echoed from the charm. "Aidan told us more about Death Valley and we freaked."

"You're going to have to give us all the details," Cass said. "Sounded rough."

"It was. Meet me at P&P. I'll brief you."

"Perfect," Cass said.

"See you in ten," Del added.

I cut the connection on the comms charm just as Connor was walking out of the kitchen with two plates piled high with cheese quiche and cheese scones.

"Thank you." I fell upon them ravenously, scarfing down Connor's magic and only barely managing to chew with my mouth closed.

"I'm noticing a trend in your food preferences," Ares said.

I shrugged, swallowing. "As far as I'm concerned, cheese makes up the base of the food pyramid."

Claire laughed. "You also think it's part of your five-a-day."

"If I believe hard enough, anything can happen. Even cheese turning into a fruit. Except that it would stay cheese." I popped the last bite of scone into my mouth and chewed.

Behind me, the door creaked open. I turned to see Cass and Del enter.

"Did you get it?" Cass asked.

"Yep. Gave the recipe to Connor ten minutes ago."

"Perfect." Cass smiled.

"Not only that, we have a lead on Drakon's location. Some place called the Valley of Darkness in Siberia."

"Sounds fun," Del said. "I've been needing a vacation."

I laughed. "It's going to be a nightmare. But at least Ademius was able to give us some info and a contact to help us. He's a guy with a serious grudge against Drakon."

"I bet there are a lot of those," Del said.

"Very likely." I nodded. "But we can head over there tomorrow. I need to rest because I feel like I've been hit by a bus, and we need to wait for Connor to finish the potion for the Vessel of Truth. I want to know what that prophecy says before we ambush Drakon."

"Smart," Del said. "I'll get Roarke."

"Aidan, too," Cass added. "If this is going to be the big showdown, we'll need backup."

"Then don't leave me out." Claire propped her hand on her hip. "Scone and coffee duty starts to wear a girl thin, you know."

"Haven't hit your demon-slaying quota for the week?" I asked.

She grinned. "Nope. And I'm starting to get itchy."

"It's settled, then," I said. "We set out tomorrow morning. Operation Catch Drakon—take two."

"Into the belly of the beast," Cass said.

"That's the truth." Ares frowned. "Siberia is no joke."

"Ever been to the Valley of Darkness?" Del asked.

Ares shook his head. "Never heard of it. But I've got a feeling it'll be a picnic."

I snorted, then punched him playfully on the shoulder. My fist moved a lot slower than I wanted it to, exhaustion weighing me down. "Right. I need to go get some shut eye."

"I'll walk you back." Ares stood.

"Okay." Did he plan to spend the night? Since I didn't want to ask in front of everyone, I kept my lips zipped and stood, joining Ares. I looked at my *deirfiúr*. "I'll see you guys in the morning. Seven, okay?"

"Sure." Cass's eyes traveled back and forth between me and Ares. She knew I liked him, but she was just now getting an inkling of how much.

As we walked out, I sent my *deirfiúr* a death glare, forbidding them from any comments, or worse, wolf whistles.

Del waggled her eyebrows. I ignored her.

Ares and I walked down the darkened street in silence. Though it was still fairly early, I was exhausted. Even if he did stay over, I'd have only enough energy to fall face first into bed.

We stopped in front of my door and I unlocked it, then stepped into the tiny foyer. Ares followed, shutting the door behind him.

He turned to face me. "I need to get back to the Vampire Realm."

"Business?" I asked. Though I knew it was a bad idea for him to sleep at my place—*two* nights in a row?—I still kind of wished he'd come over.

"Of a sort." He grinned. "I'm hungry."

"But you just—" It dawned on me then. "Oh. Blood. Right."

"Vampire."

"Of course." I opened my mouth, almost ready to suggest that he drink from me, then snapped it shut.

Idiot.

That was a huge step. Huge. And one I was not even close to ready for. So I stood on my tiptoes and pressed my lips to his. He groaned low in his throat, and then pulled me to him, his strong hands at my back.

Tension thrummed through my veins as I envisioned dragging him into my apartment and having my way with him. I wrapped my arms around his neck, wanting to climb him like a tree and wrap my legs around his waist.

His lips moved expertly on mine, warm and soft and so talented that they drove all rational thought from my mind. His hands at my back burned a hole through my clothes, warming my skin in the chill air.

I clutched him tighter, pressing my body fully against his, wanting to feel every curve and plane of hard muscle.

Ares shuddered and pulled away. "I can't, Nix."

"What?" I gasped, my blurry gaze slowly focusing on his face. "What do you mean?"

He coughed, gaze averted. "When I'm, ah, hungry, I can't do…" He gestured between us. "This. It's dangerous."

Oh. *Oh.* "Are you trying to tell me that you'll get so turned on you'll bite me?" I shivered at the idea. *Liking* it. And that wasn't exactly smart.

"It's not something I'm proud of."

"No. You're a big fan of control." I kept my hands on his shoulders so he couldn't step back.

"Exactly. And in this state, well, it's not a good idea."

"Would you, like, drain me dry?" A trill of fear skated over my skin even as my mind rejected the idea that Ares could hurt me like that. Vampires were deadly, but nothing in heaven or earth could make me believe that Ares would kill me.

"No. No." Horror crossed his face. "But I could be… too enthusiastic."

Excitement sparkled in my veins. *Oh jeez.* Was I for real? I shook my head, trying to knock some sense back into my brain.

It was a good thing he had my safety in mind, because I was an idiot. And with a guy as big and strong and fangy as him—one of us needed to not be an idiot.

"Okay then." I exhaled, stepping back. He made a good point, and as much as I might want to jump his bones, I needed to respect his wishes, too. "Night, Ares."

He kissed my cheek. The warm press of his lips nearly made me chuck my plan to take it slow and drag him in, but he disappeared a half second later, saving me from myself.

I leaned back against the wall, thumping my head against it. *I was going nuts.*

But then, I'd always been a little nuts.

Refusing to overthink things, I raced upstairs and into my apartment, heading straight for my trove. Now that Ares was gone, other desires tugged at me. The need to be amongst my preciouses was too strong to ignore.

After the stress of the last couple days, my soul desperately wanted to be in my trove. Besides the ability to find treasure, there wasn't much about me that was dragon-like. Except for my overwhelming need to sit on a pile of treasure.

I raced up the spiral staircase, taking the steps two at a time. As soon as I burst into my trove, I headed straight for the nearest table covered in plants. Though I loved my cars and weapons, it was the plants that called to me—green and vibrant and full of life.

I loved them more than ever, now, I realized. Though I'd always been drawn to them, something had awakened inside me. Just like my mother had said. All the power of Elesius flowing into me was only awakening. But it was doing it with a vengeance.

I ran my hands over the leaves and petals, gently stroking the life that I'd nurtured. My soul calmed just being here. My fingertips drifted over to the dragonfruit, one of my favorites. It was so strange with its round red and green fruit and the cactus-like stalks that held it. Light sparkled between my fingertips and the plant. I gasped. Well, that was weird.

I stared hard at the shiny green leaf. It drifted toward my hand, which I moved a few inches away. The plant leaned harder, clearly trying to reach me. Like a kitten.

So I stroked it. Comfort flowed through me. The plant seemed to sigh, though it made no noise.

"Whelp, I'm officially Poison Ivy." Except she was kinda evil, right? I'd definitely have to not go that direction. But I did need to figure out my new powers.

This was just like what happened in my dream of being a child in the forest with Ademius. That little vine had been drawn to me then, too.

A pot nearby caught my eye. The plant was withered and

dying. I hurried over, inspecting the irrigation nozzle. Something must have happened, because it was no longer releasing water.

Regret flowed through me as I petted the dying plant. It was too far gone for water and TLC to save. My heart hurt. My negligence had caused this.

Light sparkled at my fingers again, flowing into the plant. I gasped, but didn't move my hand. Before my eyes, the plant began to strengthen. The withered stalk thickened.

"Holy fates," I breathed.

It didn't come all the way back to life, but it was good enough that water might now save it. Hands shaking, I fiddled with the irrigation until water flowed.

"There you go, fella." My voice shook.

This magic was getting intense.

The comms charm around my neck crackled with power. Cass's voice followed. "Nix, uh, there's a lady here to see you."

"And she looks a hell of a lot like you," Del said. "It's your mom, isn't it?"

My heart leapt. "Maybe. I'm coming right down."

Exhaustion fled from my limbs as I raced down the stairs. Cass and Del stood outside my apartment door, my mother between them. She looked out of place in her old-school warrior gear, but she also looked like a badass. After saying goodbye to Ademius, seeing her was a balm to my soul.

"Mum!" I hugged her. She wrapped her arms around me, squeezing tight. Eventually, I stepped back. "You've met Del and Cass?"

"I have." My mother smiled at them. "We'll have to all get together sometime."

The idea was so lovely that I almost fainted. My sisters by choice and my mother. Holy fates, I was lucky.

"Why are you here?" I asked.

"I felt your magic surge and I wanted to check on you."

137

She must mean the magic that flowed between me and the plants in my trove. "You could feel that?"

"Elesius can feel it." My mother smiled. "Which means I can."

Her words triggered a memory of Moira demanding that I return. I stepped back from the door and gestured my mother inside. "Come on in. There's something I want to ask you."

"Of course." She stepped inside.

"See you later." Cass grinned, clearly happy to see me with my mother.

Del smiled, too, and waved goodbye. I shut the door behind them. My mother looked around my apartment, clearly interested but also baffled by the TV. She must not have seen many of those on her trading expeditions.

Finally, she ignored the TV and turned to me. "Are you all right? Learning to control your magic?"

"Kind of." Guilt tugged. "Well, not really. It's going to take practice. But things are happening."

"I wish I could help more." She frowned. "But you're the only one with this gift."

"Because Elesius chose me." I sat on the couch and she followed. "Why did Moira say I couldn't leave Elesius?"

"She did?" Annoyance flashed in my mother's eyes.

"Yes."

"That's ridiculous. Of course you can leave."

Hmm. Something wasn't right. I could feel it. My mother was too... off. And then there was Moira's desperation, along with the sick feeling that pervaded Elesius.

"Technically I can leave," I said. "But Moira *really* didn't want me to."

"She's just..." My mother searched for words.

Understanding dawned, clear and terrible. "The plants in that place died to give me my power. But what about the people? Will they die?"

"No." My mother shook her head, but I could see the lie in

her eyes.

"Moira was desperate for me to stay." Dread curled in my stomach. "Elesius can't survive without the plant-life. You can only trade for food for so long until your resources run out."

"We'll be fine. We can rely upon our talents."

"What? Like war? You'd become mercenaries? Sell your sword instead of the gems in the mountains."

"I don't know, Nix. But the details don't matter." My mother gripped my hand, her gaze intense. "This is not your problem. Elesius was born for sacrifice. This is our role. Just like you have yours, we have ours."

"To give everything to me. All the plant-life and the magic that keeps Elesius alive."

"It's tragic, but it doesn't matter, Nix. You must defeat Drakon. There is no way to give the magic back to Elesius. Even if you could, you shouldn't. You need that magic to defeat Drakon, and the world needs you to accomplish that."

I leaned back against the couch, sickness welling inside me. "I'm going to kill Elesius."

"Fate is going to kill Elesius," my mother said. "We've had thousands of good years. If this is the end for us, it is a noble way to go."

My throat tightened at my mother's strength and honor. I wanted to be more like her, the brave warrior who accepted her fate and strode clear-eyed into battle, no matter the cost.

Instead, I wavered, torn between what I wanted—for my city to not die because of me—and what I needed to do—defeat Drakon.

And it didn't even matter that I faltered, because she was right. I didn't know how to give the power back.

"Moira seemed to think that if I lived there, the place wouldn't die," I said.

My mother sighed. "She may be right. You are life. Your magic could sustain the place if you were there constantly."

I remembered the plant coming back to life under my fingertips. I'd done that. "If my presence can imbue a place with life, should I return to live out my days in Elesius? Would that do it?"

My heart broke just to think of it, tearing inside my chest. As much as I loved my parents and had enjoyed visiting Elesius, Magic's Bend was my home now. Ancient Magic was my life's work.

I couldn't *leave* here.

My stomach turned. But I'd have to. If I survived Drakon, I'd have to leave everything I loved so that Elesius wouldn't die.

"No." My mother's voice was sharp. "You won't sacrifice your own happiness for Elesius. If you survive Drakon—" Her voice broke, but I'd already learned my mother was too forthright and too brave to not confront the truth that I really might die on this quest "—If you survive Drakon, you will live the life that you want to live. You won't sacrifice it for Elesius."

Tears choked my throat. "You're the queen. You'd sacrifice your people?"

"I'm a mother first." Her eyes turned fierce. "A selfish one. I want your happiness above all else."

I smiled, at once both touched and horrified. "I can't be happy if everyone in Elesius dies."

She smiled, though it was sad. "I had a feeling that might be the case. Though you love it here, don't you?"

"I want to stay here above almost anything else." Just the idea of leaving my *deirfiúr*—who couldn't travel past the barrier to Elesius—made my heart shrivel in my chest.

"Don't think of it now." My mother squeezed my hand. "Focus on the task at hand, then worry about the future."

She was right. It was really the only thing I could do. It would be hard enough to defeat Drakon without extra worry dragging me down. Some might even say it was impossible.

I had a feeling it was going to take everything I had to prove them wrong.

CHAPTER TWELVE

The next morning, we all met at Potions & Pastilles promptly at seven. My mother had departed last night after our chat, and Cass and Del had immediately descended upon my apartment, questions in tow. They'd wanted to know all about her.

While I still didn't remember a lot of my past the way they did, I had an opportunity to make new memories. I'd take that any day. The three of us had fallen asleep at my place sometime around midnight.

Now, we all gathered around the bar at P&P, coffees in hand, courtesy of Claire. They'd closed P&P today so that they could help us and so there would be no observers when I untangled the prophecy using the Vessel of Truth.

Cass, Del, and I sat at barstools at the counter. Roarke, Ares, and Aidan stood behind us.

"I'll be right out!" Connor shouted from the back, where his workshop was located.

I glanced at Ares, nerves skating through me. He smiled. "It'll be all right. Perhaps the prophecy won't be bad."

I laughed. "Was that a joke?"

He smiled. "Yes."

"Even if it is a good prophecy, I bet Drakon has a plan to use it for evil."

Ares nodded. "Fair assessment."

The door from the kitchen swung open and Connor walked out, a vial full of gray potion in his hands. He held it aloft. "Ta da!"

"Looks delicious." I grimaced. Though Connor was one of the top potion makers in the world, not all of them tasted great. I opened the wooden box I'd put on the bar and removed the beaker, then handed it over to Connor. "You can pour it in here."

I held my breath as he unstoppered the bottle. Ademius had said that if we didn't get the potion right, it could destroy the beaker. I had faith in Connor, but still, it was hard to shake the nerves. So much rode on this.

Carefully, Connor poured the liquid into the vessel. When it didn't explode or shatter, the air rushed from my lungs and my shoulders relaxed. For a moment, the beaker glowed with a pale light.

"I think it worked," Cass said.

"Here's to defeating Drakon." I gave everyone one last look, then put my lips to the beaker and drank.

At first, nothing happened. It did taste worse than Connor's invisibility potion, however, which had the unfortunate flavor of mud. This was like mud plus old socks. I gagged slightly, then drained the beaker. Once the last drop was down my throat, warmth flowed through my veins. Kinda like Four Roses, but my favorite bourbon didn't come with a side of clarity and understanding. It also tasted a whole lot better.

I set the beaker on the table and closed my eyes, calling up the prophecy on instinct. The only two words that I'd understood floated in my mind— *dragons* and *return.*

Energy fizzled through my mind. I gasped, clutching the counter, as more words appeared. It was like a curtain was being drawn away. Words floated through my head.

Deep in the place where the earth meets the sun and the mist meets the magma, the Phoenix will give rise to the dragon's return or the Triumvirate will engender their fall.

I gasped, opening my eyes. "I understand the prophecy."

"What is it?" Del asked.

"Not good." My stomach turned. I met everyone's eyes. "Somehow, the three of us will be the end of the dragons."

"*Us?*" Cass's voice was stark.

"Yeah. He's not just after me. He's after all of us." My stomach twisted at the idea that Drakon wanted my *deirfiúr* as well. The stakes had been high before—but *they* were being hunted too? It shook my world. I was used to them being in dangerous situations, but this was so much bigger. I repeated the prophecy to them.

"Fall?" Del asked. "That's like... death or destruction. But they're already dead, right?"

No one had heard of or seen dragons in centuries. They'd disappeared one day, gone forever. They were assumed dead, but no one really knew. "The prophecy may be suggesting they aren't."

"If they still exist, he'll have to find them first," Ares said. "And it sounds like the prophecy gives a clue to their location."

"It's does, but it's vague." I pinched the bridge of my nose.

"*Deep in the place where the earth meets the sun and the mist meets the magma.*" Del recited the prophecy. "That sounds like it's part of a myth or something. It feels familiar, almost."

"It's another clue. One that Drakon is capable of tracking if he's given enough time." I shivered at the knowledge of how capable. He had resources and power we didn't even know about. "Maybe that's why Drakon wants us––we're supposed to help him find the dragons with our dragon sense."

"Can we?" Cass asked.

I shrugged. "We might as well try. It's not a lot to go on, but you never know."

The three of us went silent, each calling upon our dragon senses. I recalled the prophecy, using it as fuel. Seconds passed, then minutes. I pushed my magic, trying to force my dragon sense to work.

"Nothing." Del's words snapped me out of my trance.

"Same." Cass frowned.

I sighed. "Yeah. That's just not enough information to go on. But it's a place to begin. And Drakon already has a head start on us. Once he finds them, he'll do whatever terrible thing he's planning."

"If he wants to kill them, *why?*" Del asked. "There has to be something other than just the joy of doing something super evil."

The answer blazed in my mind. "Power. That has to be it, right? The dragons must be able to give him more power of some kind. Extended life or more magic or influence or something."

"It makes sense," Ares said. "And since we don't know where the dragons are to protect them, we have to kill Drakon before he finds them."

"Agreed." I looked at the clock. It was just past seven thirty. "No time like the present."

"Let's get this party started." Del grinned, but worry was clear in her eyes.

I couldn't blame her. The idea that *we* might be used to hurt dragons? Not good.

While Claire and Connor went to gather their supplies, the rest of us pulled on our winter clothes. Since we were going to Siberia in January, I figured we'd need them. We'd all agreed on black since it was going to be night when we arrived. Hopefully this would give us an element of stealth. Beneath my dark jacket I wore a black T-shirt with Basement Cat painted in dark blue. It was subtle, yet encouraging.

When Connor and Claire returned, I stepped forward. "Okay.

Cass and Ares? Could you guys transport us to the Valley of Darkness?"

Cass saluted. "I can take two at a time."

"I can do the same," Ares said. "We'll go in groups."

I reached for Ares's hand, then gestured for Claire to do the same. Aidan and Del took hold of Cass's hand.

"Ready?" Ares asked.

I nodded. A moment later, the ether sucked us in, pulling me away from the cozy warmth of P&P and spitting us out in the cold chaos of Siberia.

It took a moment for my eyes to adjust to the golden lights that shined through the gloom. I tensed. Magical signatures hit me from all sides, a cacophony of noise around me. Ares gripped my hand as people jostled around us.

As my vision cleared, I called my magic to me, ready to do battle.

But it seemed I didn't need to—not yet, at least.

We were in a magical bazaar at night. Despite the stark chill in the air, it was full of supernaturals. Not all were bundled up like we were, and I had to assume they were some variety of cold-loving species. They browsed at tented stalls selling all variety of things—food, clothing, jewelry, housewares, spells.

But the one thing that was similar amongst it all—dark magic prevailed. It stunk—a combo of garbage and rotting fish and moldy onions.

"This place stinks," I muttered.

"It's pretty though," Claire said.

She was right. Despite the foul odor of dark magic and the cold bite in the air, it did look surprisingly nice. The lights strung between the colorful tents looked like fairy lights shedding a golden glow over the wares—none of which looked as evil as they smelled. Upon closer inspection, the light bulbs were filled with sparkling glows of magic, not electricity. It was gorgeous.

The whole place looked like an enchanted evening if one could ignore the stench and prickle of evil that crept up your neck.

"Why does *everything* give off a taint of evil?" Cass asked. "Clothes, shoes, even the fruit. That's weird. Unless they're all cursed? But Curse Markets usually aren't this large."

She was right. It took a lot of power to curse items with dark magic. This place had to be the biggest Curse Market in the world.

"I'm going to go get the others," Ares said.

I let go of his hand and he disappeared. While he was gone, I called upon my dragon sense to find Torus, using what Ademius had told me about him. A faint tug pulled around my middle, directing me through the market and hopefully toward the stables.

A moment later, Ares returned with Roarke and Connor.

"You know the way?" Ares asked.

I nodded and pointed. "He's not too far."

We made our way through the market, passing by stalls of food and clothes and books. The dark magic that haunted this place never abated, but it didn't feel quite right either.

As we passed, more than one supernatural stared at us slightly too long for comfort. Fortunately, no one started anything. They knew we weren't like them, but hopefully as long as we didn't do anything shifty, they wouldn't give us any problems.

At the edge of the market, there was a corral full of horses. Some were saddled and some were not, but they were clearly meant for riding.

"Is this the parking lot?" Del asked.

"There're no cars," I said.

"I didn't see any sign of technology, actually," Claire said. "It was the stone ages back in the market. No phones, cash registers, or electric lights."

"That's weird. This place is remote, but to not even have

cars?" I inspected the paddock containing the horses, noting a large stable beyond. I pointed toward it. "I think Torus is in there."

We made our way around the paddock, finding an entrance at the side. I looked at the weathered gray wood of the door and said, "Want to bet there's no electricity in here either?"

"I'm too smart to take that bet," Del said.

Beside her, Roarke chuckled.

I pushed open the large stable door and was proven correct. It was dimly lit by several strands of the enchanted fairy lights. A long corridor led down the length, with stalls along both sides.

It wasn't heated, which was strange. Poor horses. They whinnied as we stepped inside. I headed straight for the back, following the pull of my dragon sense.

In a stall near the back, a man stood tending to a huge black horse. He rubbed a brush over the animal's hide, but stilled when I knocked on the stall door. My friends gathered at my back.

The horse looked toward me first, and I gasped at the sight of its flame-red eyes. Actual fire burned within the horse's eyes. And he had fangs.

Wow.

The man turned and frowned at me. "Who are you?"

"I'm Phoenix Knight." I considered using my given name, Lividius, but I preferred the one I'd chosen when I was fifteen. "Are you Torus?"

"I am."

"Ademius has sent me. We need to find Drakon."

The man's jaw firmed, his eyes turning wary. "Why would you want to do that?"

"I want to destroy him."

Interest glinted in his eyes. "Do you, now?"

"I'm fated to."

A slight smile tugged at his lips. "Fate, you say?"

"You don't believe in fate?" I asked.

"I once did, but now?" He shook his head, eyes sad. "If fate does exist, you'll need its help to defeat Drakon."

"Can you help us find him?"

"I can, yes."

"What will it cost?" Ares asked.

"Nothing." The man shook his head. "But I can only get you part way there, and after that, you're on your own. But if you succeed in this, I will have everything I want."

"You hate Drakon that much?"

"You have no idea." Darkness colored his voice. I could almost feel the depths of the animosity there. "If we leave now, you can be there in two hours. Can you ride?"

"Not particularly well," I said.

"We can hold on," Cass said. "This can't be that much different than a camel."

I grinned. We'd ridden camels once, through the desert. But these horses were definitely different.

"What kind of horses are these?" I asked. "They have flames for eyes and don't seem bothered by the cold." At least, I hoped they weren't bothered.

"They were once normal horses. But time has changed them. *Drakon* has changed them." Anger reddened the man's cheeks.

"How?" Ares asked.

"His influence has polluted this desert. Turned the market and everything within it dark. The horses may not mind the cold, but they no longer play as they used to. His darkness has seeped into them, stealing their joy."

Bastard. I hated Drakon. "Does this mean that this is not the biggest Curse Market in the world? That something else made it dark?"

"Exactly." Torus sighed. "Go. Meet me outside. I'll bring your rides."

We filed out of the barn, waiting in the cold night for Torus and his horses. After fifteen minutes, they filed out of the stable in a line, each fitted with black saddles and bridles.

I chose one of the smaller ones, which was still bigger than any normal horse I'd ever seen. His hooves were massive.

"His name is Flint," Torus said. "He's brave and strong. You've chosen well."

"Hi Flint." I climbed into the saddle, finding it not as difficult as I'd expected. Ares made it look like a piece of cake, though, all but leaping into the saddle. Claire and Connor were pretty good, too, no doubt all that time in their bucolic English childhood, galloping horses across the moor.

In fairness, I'd invented that childhood for them in my head. They didn't ever speak of it.

Torus walked his horse over toward me. "Ready?"

"Yep."

He led us away from the bazaar, toward the great black open of Siberia. A half moon shed light over rolling black sands of desert.

We followed in a loose cluster, like we were out for the deadliest trail ride in history. I didn't think there'd be any marshmallows roasting over an open fire.

I directed my horse toward Torus, hoping to grill him for info. Astride his horse, he looked like he could gallop through Sleepy Hollow. All he needed to do was lose his head.

I angled my horse to walk alongside his. "This is a desert. I didn't know there was one here. Aren't we at the northern edge of Siberia, near the sea?"

"We are. There shouldn't be a desert so far north, nor so close to the sea. And certainly not one like this. But it is Drakon's influence, twisting the land around his castle. Polluting it."

"That's why you hate him?"

"Yes. He destroyed my pasture, twisted my family's horses. Our magic is tied to this land, so we cannot leave. But as long as

Drakon is here, we suffer." Anger seethed in his voice as he patted the neck of the great beast he rode.

"How long has he lived there?"

"Nearly a hundred years."

A hundred years? He hadn't looked nearly that old. There was no plastic surgery that good. Which meant dark magic had to be at play, no question.

"It wasn't always this dark here, though," Torus said. "It happened over time, growing worse and worse. Our settlement won't last much longer if he doesn't leave."

Our horses climbed a great black sand dune, their wide hooves moving easily on the sand. Thunder cracked in the distance, followed by a chill wind that bit into my cheeks.

"That thunder will never bring rain." Torus's voice was edged with sadness.

"Is it his magic?"

Torus shrugged. "I think so. Things began to change when he built his castle, according to my father. It was a great operation that dug deep into the earth and dark magic spread across the land. The magic wanes when he visits, then grows when he is gone."

"What do you think that means?" Ares asked.

"I don't know." Torus shook his head. "There's a story that says he absorbs it for strength."

"So he comes here to regroup?" Del asked from behind. "How often?"

"Several times a year at least," Torus said.

"This isn't his only stronghold," I said. "We destroyed one in Oregon."

Torus grinned. "Good."

"But it was nothing like this," Cass said. "There was no well of dark magic."

"Then this is probably his home base, isn't it?" I asked. It was perfect for an evil bastard like Drakon.

"Seems like it could be." Ares pointed ahead of us. "What is that?"

There was a dark shadow ahead, filling the air.

"The Cumulus," Torus said. "Whipped up by the wind. We must go through it."

"Aren't cumulus a type of fluffy cloud?" I asked. It was rolling toward us so quickly, a dense black mass that made my stomach clench.

"Yes, but they're nothing like this." Torus's voice was strained. "This is a cloud of dark magic. Your horse will take you through, but you must help him. And whatever you do, *don't* turn back."

The cloud was almost upon us, bringing with it the overpowering stench of dark magic. The sound of a roaring wind followed it, though I felt no breeze.

"How do we help our horses?" Claire shouted over the false wind.

"You'll feel—!" Torus's words were eaten by the wind as the black cloud rushed over us. If he was going to say anything else, I couldn't hear it.

Immediately, I lost sight of my friends. Blackness closed over me, and Flint began to gallop. I clung to his back, bouncing wildly in the saddle. This was *way* harder than riding a camel. Despite Flint's speed, the darkness remained. My skin chilled. Close spaces made me cringe and this was no different.

Chill out. I sucked in a calming breath, but got nothing. No air. I gasped.

Nothing.

Oh shit.

Don't turn back. Torus's words echoed in my mind. Oh fates. My lungs burned as I clung to Flint, every atom of my being screaming to retreat. To go back to safety.

But there was no safety. There was only forward.

And I couldn't breathe.

Then Flint began to tire, stumbling as he ran. His gallop

slowed.

We're not there! I wanted to scream. My lungs ached, desperate for air.

I could feel the horse's exhaustion, feel his strength draining. Could he not breathe either?

Panic lit my mind on fire.

You can do it, Flint!

Of course the horse couldn't hear me. But he picked up his pace a tiny bit. Or maybe that was my imagination. I could still feel his misery, his exhaustion. It was like we were connected by a thread, our two souls becoming one.

I clutched the reins with one hand and pressed my hand to his neck, feeling his cool skin beneath my palm. I tried to push my magic and strength into him, praying it would help.

My muscles sagged and my brain slowed. But Flint picked up his pace. I gave him more of my strength, imagining it was a light flowing into him.

Though I was tempted to imagine that this was my new Life magic, it felt very different. I kept it up, encouraging Flint with my thoughts and my strength.

Finally, as I was beginning to lose my grip on the reins, we burst out of the blackness. I sucked in a massive breath. Nothing had ever felt so good in all my life.

I gasped as strength returned to my limbs and my lungs stopped aching. Around me, my friends plowed out of the Cumulus, gasping and choking for air. In the dim light of the moon, faces were pale and eyes stark.

"Oh my fates." Del wheezed beside me. "That was awful."

"Did you have to feed your horse your strength?" Connor asked.

"Yes," Claire said. "For a moment I thought we wouldn't make it. Then this instinct just came over me."

As I'd thought, it hadn't been my Life magic, but rather something between me and Flint. Partners.

"Fates, if I never see one of those again." Cass sounded as winded as if she'd run up a mountain.

I glanced at Ares, who looked natural upon his horse. "Cumulus huh? More like Doomulus."

A grin tugged at his mouth.

Cass laughed. "That was horrible, Nix."

Ares chuckled, and I could tell he'd liked my dumb joke. I might be going to face my potential death against an evil of unknown power, but I wasn't going to do it while moping.

"Come," Torus said. "We are close and I don't want to run into another Cumulus."

"I can get behind that," Connor said.

"Seconded," Del added.

Flint picked up the pace, trotting alongside Torus. The cold night chilled my fingers as we rode across the black desert. Eventually, the sand gave way to pastureland. The grass was as black as the sand though, and the wildflowers were navy blue and a red so deep it was almost black.

A huge castle lurked in the distance, miles away. As we rode toward it, I could just barely make out black mist hovering over the castle walls.

CHAPTER THIRTEEN

"This guy picked a proper evil lair," Claire said from the back of the group.

"He turned it evil," Torus said. "This was once my pasture. Now… no horse can eat here. Nothing can live here."

He was right. Though there was grass and flowers, I felt no sign of life. I was still unpracticed with my Life magic, but I should at least feel a hint of something.

But this was just… nothing.

Torus stopped when we were still several miles away. "This is where I must stop. I do not want any guards spotting the horses."

I couldn't blame him for playing it safe. I dismounted and gave Flint a grateful pat on the neck. "Thanks, buddy."

He whinnied, his flame-filled eyes sending a shiver down my spine. I liked him, but he sure was creepy.

"We will wait for you here," Torus said. "Six hours. After that… You are on your own."

"Thank you," Ares said.

I echoed his sentiment, then conjured a couple pots of black face paint and handed them around. "Put this on."

I wished that Connor had more invisibility potion, but we'd

used it all up at Drakon's Oregon stronghold and the new batch hadn't had time to brew. So we each painted our faces like we were Navy Seals going in to save the day, then started toward the castle, jogging through the pasture.

Soon, I was panting, regretting all the cheese sandwiches instead of salads and the runs I'd missed in favor of movies.

As we neared the castle, magic began to spark on the air. Tiny little stings pricked my skin, urging me to turn back.

Of course, we couldn't listen.

Ahead of us, jagged rocks poked out of the ground, like the earth was objecting to the presence of such dark energy and trying to repel it. The rocks circled the castle in groupings, looking almost like clusters of graves.

We were about seventy meters from the castle when magic rent the air, a shockwave of power that made my hair stand on end. Then the world lit up.

Bolts of bright red magic shot from high on the castle walls, missiles headed straight for us. They plowed into the ground all around. Immediately, I conjured a shield.

Only Claire was close to me—the others were farther ahead. I shoved my shield at her. "Take this!"

She took it and I conjured another immediately, using it to deflect a bolt of magic. It ricocheted off the shield, sending a vibration of power up my arm that shook my bones. I raced for the nearest outcropping of rock, which was still twenty meters away. My lungs burned and my skin chilled.

Jets of magic flew as we ran. Claire deflected them, racing forward. Del adopted her Phantom form, turning bright blue. No doubt she was hoping to avoid being hurt by the jets of magic. We sprinted for the rocks, becoming separated as we dodged bolts of magic. There were several clusters of rocks to hide behind—we just had to make it to them and regroup.

I avoided a blast of magic and repelled another with my shield. Ares avoided them by sheer speed, but it seemed that the jets followed us wherever we ran. I thought that we were concealed enough in the dark, but they had good vision.

A magic blast plowed into Del's leg. She stumbled, crying out and plowing into the ground. Roarke grabbed her and dragged her into his arms, shifting into his demon form in a tornado of gray light. His skin turned dark gray and his massive wings flared out behind him. He used the extra strength and speed to haul a limp Del toward the nearest outcropping of rocks, diving behind them for shelter. The stones towered ten feet above them, providing temporary cover from the blasts.

A moment later, a blast of magic hit Connor's shoulder. He stumbled, and fell. Ares diverted his path, veering toward Connor. He dragged Connor to his feet, wrapping an arm around his waist and helping him stumble toward the outcropping where Del and Roarke hid.

Though I wanted to join them, we'd become separated and they were too far away. I'd get hit before I reached them. There was another cluster of stones closer to me—they were my best bet. I hurtled toward them, nearly making it before a bolt of magic hit my shield. Power blasted me onto my back. Pain flared as I skidded on the grass.

I sucked in a ragged breath, trying to heave myself to my feet when another bolt hit me in the calf. Agony flared so bright and hot that I nearly blacked out. I doubled over, retching.

What was this dark magic?

I tried to drag myself to my feet, but the pain made my leg give out.

Footsteps thundered toward me. I twisted my head, catching sight of Cass in her griffon form. She skidded to a stop near me, kneeling so that I could clamber onto her back. It was painful, but I managed. Aidan ran beside her in his human form, deflecting bolts of magic with his own blasts of fire. Whenever his flame collided with a jet of magic, the magic deflected.

I clung to Cass's back as she galloped toward the rocks that I'd been heading for. She skidded to a stop in front of them and I fell off, leaning against the stone. She shifted quickly, returning to a size small enough that she too could hide behind the stone. Aidan joined us.

My leg burned with pain, though there was no visible damage to it. Claire skidded to a stop next to us, huddling against the rock and panting.

"Oh my fates, this is insane," she said.

Aidan bent over my leg. "Are you okay?"

"Yeah." I gasped as the pain spread. "I don't know what it is."

Aidan pressed his hand to my leg and fed healing energy into me. Warmth pushed the pain away and I sagged. Behind me, magic plowed into the stone that protected us, reverberating through the rock. It'd blast the whole thing away eventually.

I looked over at Ares and my friends. Their rocky shelter was about fifteen meters away. Ares knelt over Del and Connor, no doubt healing them with his vampire blood.

Aidan peered out from behind the rock, squinting toward the castle. He cursed and pulled back. "They have a celestial stone. It's how the magic is finding us. It's a form of remote security that is used when you don't have a lot of manpower."

"So it's directing the magic to shoot at us?" I peered around the rock. Finally, I caught sight of it, a gleaming crystal suspended halfway down the castle wall, sitting on a little ledge and contained within an iron cage. It was at least twenty feet off the ground, with the wall soaring up a total of forty feet, give or take. The magical jets were blasting off the top of the wall, firing straight for our rocks.

I ducked behind the rock. "They've got it right out in the open there."

"It needs to be able to scan the whole field."

My mind raced. "Your fireballs can knock the magic off its trajectory?"

"Yes," Aidan said. "It's just the aim that's hard. I don't always hit it."

"But you could." I looked at Cass and Aidan. "Give me some cover."

"What—"

I lunged away from the rock outcropping before Cass could finish. The problem with fighting battles alongside your loved ones was that someone was always trying to stop you from doing the dangerous things.

That included me. I wouldn't give her a chance to volunteer. And though Ares was faster than me, he was too far away and too busy healing Del and Connor.

My heart lodged in my throat as I sprinted onto the field. It was fifty meters to the castle wall. I was out in the open. Alone.

It seemed like all the magic directed itself at me. I raised my shield, deflecting a bolt that sent a shockwave streaking up my arm.

From behind me, Ares shouted. I prayed he didn't follow.

Fire shot through the air over my head, deflecting many of the jets of magic. *Thank you Cass and Aidan.*

I sprinted, lungs burning, toward the castle wall. Blasts of magic plowed into the ground around me. They slammed into my shield, nearly sending me to my knees. I pushed myself harder, only thirty meters away now.

Fewer blasts of magic plowed into the ground as Cass's and Aidan's aim improved. They were knocking more out of the sky. My plan really depended upon them providing full cover.

Twenty meters away.

A blast of magic hit my shield. I stumbled, almost falling, but pushed myself forward.

Ten meters away.

No blasts of magic hit my shield or landed near me. *Please guys, keep it up.*

Eight meters. No blasts of magic.

Seven meters. Still clear.

The celestial stone was just ahead of me, sitting on top of a little stone shelf, contained behind an iron cage.

I tossed my shield away and conjured a pole for vaulting. I shoved it into the ground, taking off with a leap. As I sailed through the air, I prayed for beginners luck.

Wind whistled by me as I flew toward the crystal. When I was near enough to grab it, I let go of the pole and reached for the stone shelf that held the shining stone.

I grabbed the edge of the shelf, hanging by one hand, and reached up to touch the crystal. I called upon my destroyer magic, letting the rushing wind soar through me and out into the crystal. Desperation drove me forward, pushing my magic into the sparkling stone. Magic sparked and shivered as the crystal fought back, but a moment later, it crumbled to dust.

The magic blasts stopped abruptly.

Holy fates. It'd worked.

But for all the effort I'd gone to, I freaking hoped it would have worked.

My arm muscles burned, reminding me that I was hanging by my fingertips twenty feet over the ground. And I was no Cliffhanger.

No surprise I hadn't thought this through all the way.

My stomach churned as I looked down, past my dangling feet toward the ground below. The fall would break my legs.

"Nix!" Ares's roar sounded from close behind me. A moment later, he stood beneath me. "I'll catch you."

Thank freaking fates, because my arms and fingertips were about to give out. I let go, dropping into Ares's arms.

He caught me without staggering, which was really quite impressive, then set me down.

"Thanks." I turned to find my friends.

They were running across the field, slower than Ares, without his vampire speed.

"You. Are. Insane." Cass scowled.

"I guess what I don't have in magic, I have to make up for in guts," I said.

"You've got guts," Del said. "No question about that."

I grinned, then turned to the wall and looked up. No guards peered down, which confirmed Aidan's theory that the security system was remotely operated by the crystal. Didn't mean there weren't other dangers past the wall, though.

"Who wants a ride?" Cass grinned and shifted into her griffon form.

Aidan followed, his golden magic bright in the dark night. He towered over Cass's smaller griffon, able to take two passengers. Claire and Connor climbed onto his back, while I scrambled onto Cass. Roarke picked Del up into his arms and spread his dark wings.

"I can climb it," Ares said.

I didn't see how that was possible, but he proved me wrong, finding toeholds and finger crevices that he used to quickly scale the wall. Cass pushed off the ground and we soared upward. She landed on the top of the wall with a thud and I scrambled off.

A shiver raced over my skin. The magic was darker here, stronger. As if we were closer to the source.

"Well, this is weird," Cass said.

"Yeah." I studied the single large tower that sat smack in the middle of the courtyard. There was nothing else within the exterior wall—no outbuildings or houses like you'd usually find inside a castle wall. Just one single tower surrounded by an open expanse stretching to the castle wall. The wall itself was circular and massively thick, at least twelve feet wide with plenty of space for an army to stand while guarding the castle. But there was no army.

"It's too empty," Ares said.

"Too quiet," Roarke added.

Which meant shit was about to get real.

The earth shook, as if it could read my thoughts. The ground surrounding the castle vibrated and shifted, packed black dirt breaking apart and rising up. Monsters—honest to god monsters of a type I'd never seen before—burst to life from the ground, born of the earth like this was some kind of crazy Greek myth.

There were three of them that I could see, each guarding a section of the empty ground, their backs to the towers. There was probably one on the far side of the tower that I couldn't see. Each was easily twenty feet tall and vaguely human shaped. Their fronts were rough gray skin, while their backs and arms were covered in long grayish white hair. Massive claws tipped each huge hand and foot, and their fangs were easily a foot long.

"Is that the Yeti?" Cass whispered.

As if he recognized his name, the one nearest to us roared. The sound pounded my eardrums, and I flinched.

"He's not as cute as the one in that claymation Christmas movie." He was downright terrifying. Not just in his size and strength, but he was ugly as Nosferatu in the sunlight. I stepped back from the wall as the beast approached. "We have to get past."

"Aidan and I can fly people over while the others defend," Cass said.

"Are you—"

The Yeti leapt for the wall, cutting off my words. His great claws gripped onto the edge and he began to pull himself up.

"Oh crap!" Cass fired a blast of flame at the Yeti's claws.

He roared and dropped back down. The other Yetis thundered over to join him, their footsteps shaking the ground.

Quickly, Cass shifted into her griffon form. Aidan followed. I lost no time in scrambling onto her back. Ares leapt onto Aidan, looking slightly uncomfortable. It was an intimate thing to ride a shifter. You got a peek into their souls in a way, and saw who they really were. Cass was my *deirfiúr* so it was no big deal, but Ares hadn't really known Aidan that long. Not that he was

LINSEY HALL

willing to let it stop him. And on the bright side, they'd probably be buddies after this.

If we survived.

Connor withdrew potion bombs from his satchel and passed them out to Claire. "Go on, we've got your back!"

Claire hurled her potion bomb at the closest Yeti. The beast roared and ducked back.

Cass and Aidan took off, pushing up into the sky. We were only about ten feet in the air when a Yeti pulled a maneuver straight from Cirque du Soleil. He bounded toward his comrade and leapt off his back, hurtling high into the air with his claws outstretched.

The massive paw slammed into Cass and Aidan, hurtling them out of the air. We flew wings over tail as we plowed toward the ground. Cass flailed her wings, only partially managing to break our fall against the hard ground.

My bones ached and my mind swam as I scrambled awkwardly to my feet. Though everything hurt, all my limbs still worked. Ares was already up, while Cass and Aidan were struggling to stand. One of Cass's wings was bent oddly, but I didn't have time to inspect it.

The Yetis had turned and were closing in, pounding toward us on massive clawed feet. From the wall, Del hurled huge icicles at them. Though most shattered off their thick hides, one managed to pierce a Yeti in the lower arm. The beast roared, swinging around to find Del.

Roarke leapt off the wall, his wings carrying him toward the Yeti. He was going for the beast's eyes, I'd bet.

Beside me, Cass shifted back to her human form.

"Go!" she cried. "We'll cover you!"

"I've got your back," Ares said.

I took one look at my friends, who planned to stay here with the deadliest beasts I'd ever seen. They were so damned brave. "Thanks."

"We're a team." Cass shrugged and hurled a massive fireball at the Yeti who was only ten feet away. The beast batted it out of the way.

Shit. This was going to be tough. I felt like I was leaving them to their deaths, but I had to find Drakon and this was our only shot.

I spun and ran for the big tower, Ares guarding my back against the Yeti who thundered after me. I didn't risk a look back until I'd reached the black door at the base of the tower. Only then did I turn to see Ares, clinging to the back of the Yeti's neck and going for the eyes. I had no idea how he'd gotten up there, but if anyone could climb a Yeti, it was Ares.

Cass hurled fireballs while Aidan fought from the sky, shooting toward the Yetis with his massive claws outstretched. Roarke dive-bombed from the air as well, landing massive blows with his fists. Connor and Claire hurled potion bombs while Del threw her icicles.

Badasses. Every one of them.

I turned back to the door and pushed it open, slipping inside the darkened tower. It took a moment for my eyes to adjust. The tower was empty and dark, the ceiling soaring high above. It was so hot in here compared to the cold Siberian night that I had to throw off my jacket. The sight of my Basement Cat T-shirt underneath gave me a little boost of confidence.

And I was going to need it, because the magic was darkest here, and strongest. And my dragon sense was going wild. It pulled toward the floor, as if Drakon were down there.

I scanned the room for a door and found a dark spot on the ground across the tower. A stairway?

I hurried over, keeping my footsteps as quiet as possible. It *was* a door, built right into the ground. I pulled open the hatch and found a set of stone stairs that went straight into hell.

CHAPTER FOURTEEN

My heart lodged in my throat as I crept down the stairs. The dark magic gagged me as I descended, making my eyes water and the inside of my mouth feel greasy from trying to breathe through my mouth instead of my nose.

Though it was dark down here, an orange glow from the bottom of the stairs lit my way. At the base, I peered into the main room and gasped.

It was as big as the tower above, but that's where the similarities ended. In the middle, a pool of an oily black substance sat stagnant and threatening. All around the edges, terrifying black vines covered the ground, growing out of the pool.

I'd never met a plant I didn't like, but there was a first time for everything.

Overhead, a massive black chandelier was filled with dark candles that glowed with orange light. I squinted, trying to figure out where Drakon was hiding.

It wasn't until the dark oil rippled slightly that I realized he was *in* the black pond. That's where the black magic was coming from, so that's where he was. It was hard to see him because he was fully coated in the black muck and floating quietly, but he was definitely there.

Taking some kind of evil, super villain bath.

It should have made him less intimidating, but it did the opposite. Anyone who could stay submerged in that muck—who enjoyed it—was too evil for my taste.

I conjured a bow and arrow, trying my damnedest to keep my magical signature on low so he couldn't sense me. The bow and arrow appeared in my hands. I drew a silent, steady breath and raised the bow, then nocked the arrow.

I sighted the floating body, which was definitely alive or my dragon sense wouldn't have gotten so excited, and aimed the arrow. As I released the string, I prayed to fate.

The arrow sailed straight and true toward Drakon's chest. Right before it plunged inside, he burst from the oil in a splash of black fluid and knocked the arrow aside.

Shit.

"How dare you?" His roar was an unholy sound. Not even human.

Icy shivers raced across my skin.

He floated in midair, his form dripping the oily muck back into the pond. How the hell was he *floating*?

I could barely make out his features through the oil, but slowly it slid off his face to reveal the man I'd seen at the compound in Oregon.

I conjured another arrow, wishing I had more magic than I did. Didn't matter, though. No way I was running back up those stairs.

So I fired, aiming straight for his heart. Again, he batted the arrow away. I drew again. Before I could fire, he surged toward me, throwing a sonic boom that blasted me off my feet.

I slammed back against the stairs, pain singing through my back. Everything hurt as I dragged myself to my feet and conjured a shield. It would be wholly insufficient, but it was all I had.

As he raised his hand to throw another blast, I looked frantically around the room, trying to find anything I could use to my advantage.

The only thing I could think of was tossing a stick of dynamite into the oil and hoping it was as flammable as it looked. That'd blow me up too, but since I would probably die here anyway, I was willing to do it. I didn't know if my friends were in the tower above, though. Or if the blast would take out the whole castle. I couldn't risk them as well.

The debate took me too long. Draken hurled another sonic boom at me. I blocked it with my shield, but crashed back into the wall all the same, pain enveloping me as my insides felt like they liquified. My vision blurred as I gasped for air.

"You thought to disturb me?" Drakon roared. "To destroy me?"

"The second one." The words hurt just coming out.

Drakon threw another blast at me, this one stronger than all the rest. Since I hadn't managed to remove myself from the wall that I'd been flattened against, it hit me dead on, all the force going straight into my middle.

I coughed, tasting blood.

Internal damage.

He was stronger than he'd been back at the compound in Oregon, or he'd have used this against me. No doubt it was from the dark evil here—he really was absorbing it for his own.

And I was here to fight him with just a shield and my bow. My clever tricks wouldn't work when my friends were at risk. *When in doubt, blow it up* did not apply in this circumstance. I had plant magic, but didn't know how to use it. Not that these dark plants could help me.

The blast of the sonic boom took its toll. I slid to my knees, unable to stand. The dark vines beneath me broke my fall, but they didn't feel alive like normal plants.

Boy, I'd really gotten myself into it this time.

"How could I be threatened by a coward—a weakling like you?" he roared.

"The second one," I choked out.

"What?" he roared.

"I'm the second, not the first." Cowardice had never been my issue.

That seemed to enrage him even more. His dark magic pulsed from him, filling the air with a horrible burning sensation. Fates, he was awful. Drakon slammed another burst of magic into me.

I was nothing but a mass of pain and pulverized organs, so I barely felt it. But I keeled over anyway, my face pressing against the dark vines.

Holy fates, this guy was so much stronger than I'd expected. Out of this world strong.

He floated down from the air, landing on the edge of the pool twenty feet away. I lay still, dying, as he slowly approached.

Did he want to deliver the killing blow while looking into my eyes or something? Like some creepy serial killer in a bad TV movie?

What a way to go.

Just the idea made me die a little inside. Like an appetizer for the main course. This couldn't be the end for me... caught by surprise and killed by some evil bastard who'd just gotten out of his bath. The indignity was too much to bear.

I'd fight. Somehow—even if I couldn't move.

Beneath me, the vines trembled, as if they'd heard my vow. Slowly, they began to leech energy into me. I couldn't tell what it was at first, but the warmth was unmistakable. It flowed through me, warm and strong, heating my insides as it mended me. There was a darkness to it—no doubt because the vines grew out of the pool of oil. But they also gave me strength. Healing strength. The magic awed me, shaking me to my marrow.

Except it was slow. Far too slow.

Drakon was only ten feet away now. Eight feet. He'd strike any moment now and I couldn't even stand.

Help! I was still too broken to speak, but it didn't stop my mind from trying. All I needed was a little time. Just a few moments. If only my friends would come and hold him off until I could take him out once and for all.

Red blurs shot from the stairwell and into the room, drawing my eyes. Shock blanked out my mind, but it was unmistakable.

The Pūķis.

Somehow, they'd made it out of the Vampire Realm and found me when I needed them. My friends *had* come—just not the ones I'd expected.

The Pūķis dived for Drakon, blasting fire his way. He turned to them, rage twisting his features, and hit them with his sonic boom. One Pūķi took a direct hit, bowling backward toward the wall.

No! My insides tore as the Pūķi struggled to rise.

Rage filled me with fire as Drakon tried to hurt my friends. The Pūķi were fast and fierce, landing their fiery blows upon his flesh. But it only seemed to enrage him more. He threw blast after blast at them. Though they swooped and dived, they couldn't dodge them all.

I gripped the vines at my sides and drew the energy from them. I turned the slow, passive process into one that I controlled. Building my strength, healing my body.

And the best part was, I could feel the vines' joy. I wasn't killing them by taking their energy. I was healing them. My touch was driving away Drakon's darkness.

Soon, I could move my arms. Then my legs. As the Pūķi drew Drakon's fire, I healed, finally rising to my feet, the vines at my side. They were a deep, dark green as they rose up around me like snakes.

Power filled my chest to bursting.

"Drakon!" I roared, calling his attention away from the Pūķis.

He spun to face me, jaw slackening. I grinned, feeling the power flowing through my veins as the vines waved at my side, ready to strike.

They felt like they were one with me. Which they were. Their life was inside me and mine was inside them. Power roared through me like a tornado, so much better than that miserable destroyer magic I'd taken from Aleric.

This was true power. This was life.

And I'd use it to create death.

Just one death, but I knew it would save so many others. It quashed any guilt I might have had.

I threw my hands out toward Drakon. The vines followed the motion, surging toward him like synchronized snakes. They wrapped around him from head to toe, encapsulating him fully. Determination welled within me as I yanked my hands apart.

The vines did the same, tearing Drakon to pieces. Ripping him limb from limb. Victory surged through me, warm and bright. I'd done it!

A fraction of a second later, a massive black cloud exploded up from the vines that contained Drakon's destroyed body. It was inky and dark, nearly opaque. Evil radiated from it—pure and unadulterated. Stronger than anything I'd ever felt. It coalesced to form a massive dragon made of smoke. The beast roared, a sound that shook my very bones and made me stumble back onto my butt.

Then the beast rushed away, flying up through the ceiling in a burst of energy.

Oh, shit.

I blinked, staring up at the unharmed ceiling, my mind scrambling for answers. I didn't know what the hell that thing had been, but one thing was for sure.

I hadn't beaten Drakon. Not by a long shot.

Footsteps sounded on the stairs. I shifted. My friends piled into the room, weapons drawn.

Ares's eyes fell upon me. "Nix! Are you all right?"

They hurried toward me as I struggled to my feet. The Pūķi flew over, all of them fine except for one who wobbled a bit when he flew. I hoped he'd get better.

"What happened?" Cass demanded.

I swayed on my feet, still shocked by what I'd seen. What I'd done.

Del's eyes landed on the body that I'd torn apart. "You got him!"

"Uh." I looked around, my mind still struggling to comprehend what had happened. "I didn't."

"What do you mean?" Ares asked.

"That man—the mob boss guy—he wasn't Drakon."

"What?" Del frowned.

"Drakon was *inside* of him. I killed the body, but not the monster. Not our true enemy." My mind scrambled, remembering what I'd seen. "And... he was a dragon made of black smoke."

"Is that what rushed out of the tower roof?" Claire asked.

"Yes."

"Damn." Connor shook his head. "As soon as that thing flew away, the Yetis collapsed back into the ground. Those things were impossible to take out."

That's why my friends had appeared as soon as Drakon had gone. They'd been fighting the Yetis all this time.

"You've weakened him, though," Ares said. "He wanted that body. Now he doesn't have it."

"Yeah." I recalled the sheer crazy black magic that had

emanated from the shadow dragon. "But not for long. He's *strong*. And really freaking evil."

"Then we need to destroy this place," Roarke said. "It's where he refuels his power."

"Yes." I nodded vehemently. "Absolutely."

But how? I studied the room. The problem wasn't the castle itself. I could blow that up with some dynamite, no problem. It was the pool of evil black oil that had me worried. It was as if Drakon had managed to liquefy evil energy and turn it into a battery.

We couldn't just blow the oil up. It would splatter everywhere, sinking back into the earth.

The memory of the celestial stone turning to dust flashed in my mind's eye. If only I could destroy the oil the same way. But I'd never managed to destroy something so big. I'd need more power. More energy.

My eye caught on the vines growing out of the oil and I remembered the magical energy leaching from the vines into me. They'd drawn that energy from the oil. It'd been a dark energy, but it'd been energy all the same.

"I think I can destroy the oil." I swallowed hard, dreading what was to come.

"How?" Ares asked.

I didn't answer, afraid they would tell me it was too dangerous. I stepped toward the edge of the pool and knelt on the vines. They cushioned my knees as I knelt forward and touched my fingertip to the oil.

Sickness flowed into me, making me gag.

"Don't touch that!" Cass cried.

I ignored her, reaching my other hand into the vines and burying it deep among them. Energy fizzled up my hand. I imagined myself absorbing it. Becoming one with the vines.

Thank you. The vines understood me. I could feel it.

They fed me their energy. It wasn't as dark as the oil I was touching, but it still made me queasy to absorb so much of it. As it filled me, I called on my destroyer power. It surged up inside me, a rushing wind that roared its pleasure at the dark magic filling my being.

I fed the destructive power into the oil. It was the perfect circle––the vines took their energy from the oil, which I turned into destruction and fed back into the oil.

Too bad it felt like hell. I gasped as the sickness rose inside me, black tar drowning my organs. But I didn't stop feeding the magic into the oil.

I stared at my fingertip submerged in the oil, watching as the shining black liquid turned dull and dry. The destruction spread out from my fingertip, turning the gleaming surface to dull gray dust. Then even that began to crumble away, disappearing.

My muscles trembled as I worked, my stomach turning. Being a conduit for this much dark magic was making me ill. It took everything I had to remain kneeling.

The vines began to feed me less and less magic as the oil disappeared. Finally, there was nothing left but an empty pool covered by a fine layer of dust.

I sagged, struggling to catch my breath.

Ares dropped to his knees beside me, wrapping an arm around my waist. "Are you all right?"

"I'm okay." I straightened.

"That was amazing," Cass said.

"Incredible," Del added.

Around me, the vines began to shrivel and die. My heart tugged and my chest felt heavy as I looked at them. "I'm really sorry, guys."

"Who are you talking to?" Ares asked.

"The vines." A smile tugged at my lips. "I've got some seriously badass powers, apparently. But they made a great sacrifice for me."

"Then they deserve our thanks," Ares said.

I smiled, pleased that he got on board with thanking plants. I knew it was a little nuts, but it was *my* nuts.

I struggled to rise, swaying slightly on my feet as the sickness from the dark magic polluted my insides. "It's time to get the hell out of here."

"I couldn't agree more," Cass said.

I leaned on Ares as I followed my friends out of the horrible room, the Pūķi at my side. The wobbly one was flying a bit better already, thankfully.

"How the hell did you get them out of the Vampire Realm?" Ares asked as we walked across the main tower room.

I grabbed my jacket off the ground and shrugged it on. "I have no idea. We're buddies."

"Being buddies doesn't mean you can defy the laws of the supernatural world."

"Apparently it does." I stepped out into the cold, shoulders tensed. But the Yetis were still under the dirt, thank fates. I turned to Cass. "I want to destroy the castle itself, and I've got a plan, but I'll need a ride."

She saluted. "Sure thing, Cap."

I grinned. "Everyone needs to get far away from here. Then get ready for the fireworks."

Ares clearly didn't want to let me go, but I pressed hard on his arm to remove it from my waist. "I'll be okay, I promise. I've got Cass."

He gave me a skeptical look. "You look ill."

"I don't feel so hot from the dark magic, but really—Cass will take care of me. And you can't be here when I light this place up."

Finally, he nodded and stepped back. "Be careful."

Cass shifted into her griffon form as my other friends got the hell out of the castle the way we'd entered. I climbed on top of Cass's back and she pushed off into the air. From above, I could see everyone sprinting away from the castle, toward Torus and the waiting horses.

"Take us above the tower!" I cried, watchful of the air around us. I didn't know what Drakon was capable of in his truest form, but I didn't want to find out right now.

Cass flew us over the top of the tower and hovered about fifty meters above. Once everyone was far enough away, I held my hand out over the air and called upon Old Faithful, my conjuring magic. I was well tapped out of destroyer magic right now. I needed something easy and reliable.

I envisioned a massive boulder as big as Fabio. It formed in the air right under my palm, then plummeted toward the tower. With a crash, it plowed through the roof and then through the floor below, revealing Drakon's horrible pit to the world. At least it was empty of the oil. Soon, he wouldn't even be able to refill the pool. His whole place would be gone.

I held my breath and conjured several large sticks of dynamite. I lit them with a conjured match, then dropped them toward the hole the boulder had created. They'd blow up from within, causing the ultimate destruction.

"Go!" I cried.

Cass took off, hurtling toward safety.

A massive boom rent the air and I turned, watching the fiery explosion tear the castle apart. I turned back as Cass flew us toward our friends. I clung to her back, wind tearing at my hair. I couldn't believe what had just happened. The bad... The good. And the magic that I'd wielded... it had been phenomenal.

CHAPTER FIFTEEN

The next night, after we'd all recovered from the expedition to Siberia, we decided to do something totally crazy.

We threw a dinner party.

Because of size restrictions, we had to host it at Ares's house, which was the only place big enough for all of us.

"This was an excellent idea," Ares said as he mixed the queso and chiles together.

"Everyone needs to eat." I dumped chips into a bowl. "And everyone needs a break. Even if it is a short one."

Cass, who leaned against the granite counter, raised her can of PBR. "Couldn't agree more."

I grinned and took a sip of my Four Roses, enjoying the burn. Bourbon was perfect for situations like this. "And we're not technically taking the evening off. We're just having our wrap-up with some food and a view."

"And what a view it is." Connor hiked his thumb back toward the living room where the expansive windows gave the incredible view of Magic's Bend at night. "You sure know how to live, Ares."

"Um, thank you," Ares said, clearly off kilter with compliments on his fancy apartment. He might not think it was fancy, but we sure did.

"I think we're ready." I picked up the bowl of chips and headed toward the living room. "Grab the queso, please."

Ares picked up the bowl and followed us out. Claire, Del, and Roarke sat on the gray couches, chatting. We joined them, setting the food down on the table. The main courses would come later, but for now, we'd take care of business.

We hadn't seen each other since our ride back across the desert and the return to Magic's Bend last night, since everyone had needed some medical care and a good long sleep. It'd taken me last night and today to recover from the dark magic that had surged through me, but I was starting to improve a bit. I was still haunted by the idea that I'd have to return and live in Elesius if I didn't want my homeland to die, but I was trying to ignore that worry. First things first, and all that.

"Thanks for your help, guys." I smiled. "You made all the difference, keeping those Yetis off my back. Not to mention all the rest."

"Always." Cass raised her PBR. "Here's to deadly adventures."

I raised my glass, enjoying the glint of light on the amber liquid. We clinked our glasses together.

"Torus was so happy about the destruction of the castle," Claire mused. "I've never seen a man so gleeful."

Joy warmed my chest. "He was, wasn't he?"

"As for Drakon," Ares said. "He's still out there."

"And we have no new clues about his location." Del frowned. "Or why he wants to kill the dragons. What does he hope to gain?"

"No idea. If only our FireSoul magic was strong enough to find him." I'd been trying all day with no luck.

"Whatever concealment charm he's wearing is powerful," Cass said. "I don't think we're going to have a breakthrough on that."

"We could try to find the dragons," Connor said. "Though the prophecy was pretty vague."

"Aren't they usually?" Claire laughed.

She had a point. Prophecies were often hard to understand even if you did know the whole thing.

"It's a clue, at least." I clung to that hope. "We just need more clues. Drakon will hunt them. So we will too. And you never know, Drakon might come to us. He needs us for his plan."

"We could make ourselves bait." Cass grinned, a cunning glint in her eye.

"Something like that," I said.

"I don't like it," Ares said. "Too dangerous."

"I second that." Roarke's words tripped over Aidan's, which were basically identical.

I looked at Ares. "We're used to dangerous. It's kind of what we do."

"I've noticed that," he said.

"Good." I nodded. "We'll come up with a plan. Because Drakon is coming for us. And we have to be ready."

~

Across Town...

Inside Nix's trove, magic sparked, illuminating the darkness. Plants rustled with magic, as if they sensed the change in the air. The dragonfruit plant shivered as magic flowed through its stalks and fruit. It shifted, morphing with the magic of Life. The magic of FireSouls.

As rain pattered on the glass ceiling of the greenhouse, one of the fat round dragonfruits dropped from the stalk and landed in the dirt. Power vibrated through it, and the fruit took on new life. It stretched and unfurled, growing limbs, then a tail, and finally a head. Red scales tipped with green glinted in the light of the moon that flooded through the glass ceiling. Green wings and obsidian claws curled against the dragon's small body.

Thunder cracked in the distance as the tiny dragon—born of magic and life—opened its dark eyes and sought the future.

~~~

Nix's next book, *Enemy of Magic,* is now available. Click here to get it or turn the page for an excerpt.

Or, get a free copy of *Hidden Magic* and learn how the *deirfiúr* got started in the treasure hunting business, sign up for my newsletter. No spam, and you can unsubscribe any time.

THANK YOU FOR READING!

I hope you enjoyed reading this book as much as I enjoyed writing it. Reviews are *so* helpful to authors. I really appreciate all reviews, both positive and negative. If you want to leave one, you can do so on Amazon or GoodReads

Turn the page for an excerpt of *Hidden Magic*, which you can get for free in ebook form by signing up for my mailing list at www.linseyhall.com/subscribe.

EXCERPT OF HIDDEN MAGIC

(Told from the perspective of Cass Clereaux)

Jungle, Southeast Asia
  Five years before the events in Demon Magic

"How much are we being paid for this job again?" I asked as I glanced at the inhabitants filling the bar. It was a motley crowd of supernaturals, many of whom looked shifty as hell.

"Not nearly enough." Del frowned at the man across the bar, who was giving her his best sexy face. There was a lot of eyebrow movement happening. "Is he having a seizure?"

"Looks like it." Nix grinned. "Though I gotta say, I wasn't expecting this. We're basically in a tree, for magic's sake. In the middle of the jungle! Where are all these dudes coming from?"

"According to my info, there's a mining operation near here. Though I'd say we're more *under* a tree than *in* a tree."

"I'm with Cass," Del said. "Under, not in."

"Fair enough." Nix's green eyes traveled around the room.

We were deep in Southeast Asia, in a bar that had long ago

been reclaimed by the jungle. A massive fig tree had grown over and around the ancient building, its huge roots encapsulating the stone walls. It was straight out of a fairy tale. Monks had once lived here, but a few supernaturals of indeterminate species had gotten ahold of it and turned it into a watering hole for the local supernaturals. We were meeting our local contact here, but he was late.

"Hey, pretty lady." A smarmy voice sounded from my left. "What are you?"

I turned to face the guy who was giving me the up and down, his gaze roving from my tank top to my shorts. He wasn't Clarence, our local contact. And if he meant "what kind of supernatural are you?" I sure as hell wouldn't be answering.

"Not interested is what I am," I said.

"Aww, that's no way to treat a guy." He grasped my hip, rubbing his thumb up and down.

I gagged, then smacked his hand away, tempted to throat-punch him. It was a favorite move of mine, but I didn't want to start a fight before Clarence got here. Didn't want to piss off the boss and all. He liked it when jobs went smoothly.

The man raised his hands. "Hey, hey. No need to get feisty. You three sisters?"

I glanced doubtfully at Nix and Del, with their dark hair that was so different from my red. We might call ourselves sisters— *deirfiúr* in our native Irish—but this idiot didn't know that. We were all about twenty years old, but we looked nothing alike.

"Go away," I said. I had no patience for dudes who touched me within a second of saying hello. "Run along and flirt with your hand, because that's all the action you'll be getting tonight."

His face turned a mottled red, and he raised a fist. His magic welled, the scent of rotten fruit overwhelming.

He thought he was going to smack me? Or use his magic against me?

I lashed out, punching him in the throat as I'd wanted to

earlier. His eyes bulged and he gagged. I kneed him in the crotch, grinning when he keeled over.

"Hey!" A burly man with a beard lunged for us, his buddy beside him following. "That's no way—"

"To treat a guy?" I finished for him as I kicked out at him. My tall, heavy boots collided with his chest, sending him flying backward. I might not use my magic, but I sure as hell could fight.

His friend raised his hand and sent a blast of wind at us. It threw me backward, sending me skidding across the floor.

By the time I'd scrambled to my feet, a brawl had broken out in the bar. Fists flew left and right, with a bit of magic thrown in. Nothing bad enough to ruin the bar, like jets of flame, because no one wanted to destroy the only watering hole for a hundred miles, but enough that it lit up the air with varying magical signatures.

Nix conjured a baseball bat and swung it at a guy who charged her, while Del teleported behind a man and smashed a chair over his head. I'd always been jealous of Del's ability to sneak up on people like that.

All in all, it was turning into a good evening. Watching a fight between supernaturals was fun.

"Enough!" the bartender bellowed, right before I could throw myself back into the fray. "Or no more beer!"

The bar settled down immediately. I glared at the jerk who'd started it. There was no way I'd take the blame, even though I'd thrown the first punch. He should have known better.

The bartender gave me a look and I shrugged, hiking a thumb at the jerk who'd touched me. "He shoulda kept his hands to himself."

"Fair enough," the bartender said.

I nodded and turned to find Nix and Del. They'd grabbed our beers and were putting them on a table in the corner. I went to join them.

We were a team. Sisters by choice, ever since we'd woken in a field at fifteen with no memories other than those that said we were FireSouls on the run from someone who had hurt us. Who was hunting us.

Our biggest goal, even bigger than getting out from under our current boss's thumb, was to save enough money to buy concealment charms that would hide us from the monster who hunted us. He was just a shadowy memory, but it was enough to keep us running.

"Where is Clarence, anyway?" I pulled my damp tank top away from my sweaty skin. The jungle was damned hot. We couldn't break into the temple until Clarence gave us the information we needed to get past the guard at the front. And we didn't need to spend too much longer in this bar.

Del glanced at her watch, her blue eyes flashing with annoyance. "He's twenty minutes late. Old Man Bastard said he should be here at eight."

Old Man Bastard—OMB for short—was our boss. His name said it all. Del, Nix, and I were FireSouls, the most despised species of supernatural because we could steal other magical being's powers if we killed them. We'd never done that, of course, but OMB didn't care. He'd figured out our secret when we were too young to hide it effectively and had been blackmailing us to work for him ever since.

It'd been four years of finding and stealing treasure on his behalf. Treasure hunting was our other talent, a gift from the dragon with whom legend said we shared a soul. No one had seen a dragon in centuries, so I wasn't sure if the legend was even true, but dragons were covetous, so it made sense they had a knack for finding treasure.

"What are we after again?" Nix asked.

"A pair of obsidian daggers," Del said. "Nice ones."

"And how much is this job worth?" Nix repeated my earlier question. Money was always on our minds. It was our only chance at buying our freedom, but OMB didn't pay us enough for it to be feasible anytime soon. We kept meticulous track of our earnings and saved like misers anyway.

"A thousand each."

"Damn, that's pathetic." I slouched back in my chair and stared up at the ceiling, too bummed about our crappy pay to even be impressed by the stonework and vines above my head.

"Hey, pretty ladies." The oily voice made my skin crawl. We could just not get a break in here. I looked up to see Clarence, our contact.

Clarence was a tall man, slender as a vine, and had the slicked back hair and pencil-thin mustache of a 1940s movie star. Unfortunately, it didn't work on him. Probably because his stare was like a lizard's. He was more Gomez Addams than Clark Gable. I'd bet anything that he liked working for OMB.

"Hey, Clarence," I said. "Pull up a seat and tell us how to get into the temple."

Clarence slid into a chair, his movement eerily snakelike. I shivered and scooted my chair away, bumping into Del. The scent of her magic flared, a clean hit of fresh laundry, as she no doubt suppressed her instinct to transport away from Clarence. If I had her gift of teleportation, I'd have to repress it as well.

"How about a drink first?" Clarence said.

Del growled, but Nix interjected, her voice almost nice. She had the most self control out of the three of us. "No can do, Clarence. You know... Mr. Oribis"—her voice tripped on the name, probably because she wanted to call him OMB—"wants the daggers soon. Maybe next time, though."

"Next time." Clarence shook his head like he didn't believe her. He might be a snake, but he was a clever one. His chest puffed up a bit. "You know I'm the only one who knows how to get into the temple. How to get into any of the places in this jungle."

"And we're so grateful you're meeting with us. Mr. Oribis is so grateful." Nix dug into her pocket and pulled out the crumpled envelope that contained Clarence's pay. We'd counted it and found—unsurprisingly—that it was more than ours combined, even though all he had to do was chat with us for two minutes. I'd wanted to scream when I'd seen it.

Clarence's gaze snapped to the money. "All right, all right."

Apparently his need to be flattered went out the window when cash was in front of his face. Couldn't blame him, though. I was the same way.

"So, what are we up against?" I asked.

The temple containing the daggers had been built by supernaturals over a thousand years ago. Like other temples of its kind, it was magically protected. Clarence's intel would save us a ton of time and damage to the temple if we could get around the enchantments rather than breaking through them.

"Dvarapala. A big one."

"A gatekeeper?" I'd seen one of the giant, stone monster statues at another temple before.

"Yep." He nodded slowly. "Impossible to get through. The temple's as big as the Titanic—hidden from humans, of course— but no one's been inside in centuries, they say."

Hidden from humans was a given. They had no idea supernaturals existed, and we wanted to keep it that way.

"So how'd you figure out the way in?" Del asked. "And why *haven't* you gone in? Bet there's lots of stuff you could fence in there. Temples are usually full of treasure."

"A bit of pertinent research told me how to get in. And I'd rather sell the entrance information and save my hide. It won't be easy to get past the booby traps in there."

Hide? Snakeskin, more like. Though he had a point. I didn't think he'd last long trying to get through a temple on his own.

"So? Spill it," I said, anxious to get going.

He leaned in, and the overpowering scent of cologne and sweat hit me. I grimaced, held my breath, then leaned forward to hear his whispers.

***

As soon as Clarence walked away, the communications charms around my neck vibrated. I jumped, then groaned. Only one person had access to this charm.

I shoved the small package Clarence had given me into my short's pocket and pressed my fingertips to the comms charm, igniting its magic.

"Hello, Mr. Oribis." I swallowed my bile at having to be polite.

"Girls," he grumbled.

Nix made a gagging face. We hated when he called us girls.

"Change of plans. You need to go to the temple tonight."

"What? But it's dark. We're going tomorrow." He never changed the plans on us. This was weird.

"I need the daggers sooner. Go tonight."

My mind raced. "The jungle is more dangerous in the dark. We'll do it if you pay us more."

"Twice the usual," Del said.

A tinny laugh echoed from the charm. "Pay *you* more? You're lucky I pay you at all."

I gritted my teeth and said, "But we've been working for you for four years without a raise."

"And you'll be working for me for four more years. And four after that. And four after that." Annoyance lurked in his tone. So did his low opinion of us.

Del's and Nix's brows crinkled in distress. We'd always suspected that OMB wasn't planning to let us buy our freedom, but he'd dangled that carrot in front of us. What he'd just said made that seem like a big fat lie, though. One we could add to the many others he'd told us.

An urge to rebel, to stand up to the bully who controlled our lives, seethed in my chest.

"No," I said. "You treat us like crap, and I'm sick of it. Pay us fairly."

"I treat you like *crap*, as you so eloquently put it, because that is exactly what you are. *FireSouls.*" He spit the last word, imbuing it with so much venom I thought it might poison me.

I flinched, frantically glancing around to see if anyone in the bar had heard what he'd called us. Fortunately, they were all distracted. That didn't stop my heart from thundering in my ears as rage replaced the fear. I opened my mouth to shout at him, but snapped it shut. I was too afraid of pissing him off.

"Get it by dawn," he barked. "Or I'm turning one of you in to the Order of the Magica. Prison will be the least of your worries. They might just execute you."

I gasped. "You wouldn't." Our government hunted and imprisoned—or destroyed—FireSouls.

"Oh, I would. And I'd enjoy it. The three of you have been more trouble than you're worth. You're getting cocky, thinking you have a say in things like this. Get the daggers by dawn, or one of you ends up in the hands of the Order."

My skin chilled, and the floor felt like it had dropped out from under me. He was serious.

"Fine." I bit off the end of the word, barely keeping my voice from shaking. "We'll do it tonight. Del will transport them to you as soon as we have them."

"Excellent." Satisfaction rang in his tone, and my skin crawled. "Don't disappoint me, or you know what will happen."

The magic in the charm died. He'd broken the connection.

I collapsed back against the chair. In times like these, I wished I had it in me to kill. Sure, I offed demons when they came at me on our jobs, but that was easy because they didn't actually die. Killing their earthly bodies just sent them back to their hell.

But I couldn't kill another supernatural. Not even OMB. It might get us out of this lifetime of servitude, but I didn't have it in me. And what if I failed? I was too afraid of his rage—and the consequences—if I didn't succeed.

"Shit, shit, shit." Nix's green eyes were stark in her pale face. "He means it."

"Yeah." Del's voice shook. "We need to get those daggers."

"Now," I said.

"I wish I could just conjure a forgery," Nix said. "I really don't want to go out into the jungle tonight. Getting past the Dvarapala in the dark will suck."

Nix was a conjurer, able to create almost anything using just her magic. Massive or complex things, like airplanes or guns, were outside of her ability, but a couple of daggers wouldn't be hard.

Trouble was, they were a magical artifact, enchanted with the ability to return to whoever had thrown them. Like boomerangs. Though Nix could conjure the daggers, we couldn't enchant them.

"We need to go. We only have six hours until dawn." I grabbed my short swords from the table and stood, shoving them into the holsters strapped to my back.

A hush descended over the crowded bar.

I stiffened, but the sound of the staticky TV in the corner made me relax. They weren't interested in me. Just the news, which was probably being routed through a dozen techno-witches to get this far into the jungle.

The grave voice of the female reporter echoed through the quiet bar. "The FireSoul was apprehended outside of his apartment in Magic's Bend, Oregon. He is currently in the custody of the Order of the Magica, and his trial is scheduled for tomorrow morning. My sources report that execution is possible."

I stifled a crazed laugh. Perfect timing. Just what we needed to hear after OMB's threat. A reminder of what would happen if he turned us into the Order of the Magica. The hush that descended over the previously rowdy crowd—the kind of hush you get at the scene of a big accident—indicated what an interesting freaking topic this was. FireSouls were the bogeymen. *I* was the bogeyman, even though I didn't use my powers. But as long as no one found out, we were safe.

My gaze darted to Del and Nix. They nodded toward the door. It was definitely time to go.

As the newscaster turned her report toward something more boring and the crowd got rowdy again, we threaded our way between the tiny tables and chairs.

I shoved the heavy wooden door open and sucked in a breath of sticky jungle air, relieved to be out of the bar. Night creatures screeched, and moonlight filtered through the trees above. The jungle would be a nice place if it weren't full of things that wanted to kill us.

"We're never escaping him, are we?" Nix said softly.

"We will." Somehow. Someday. "Let's just deal with this for now."

We found our motorcycles, which were parked in the lot with a dozen other identical ones. They were hulking beasts with massive, all-terrain tires meant for the jungle floor. We'd done a lot of work in Southeast Asia this year, and these were our favored forms of transportation in this part of the world.

Del could transport us, but it was better if she saved her power. It wasn't infinite, though it did regenerate. But we'd learned a long time ago to save Del's power for our escape. Nothing worse than being trapped in a temple with pissed off guardians and a few tripped booby traps.

We'd scouted out the location of the temple earlier that day, so we knew where to go.

I swung my leg over Secretariat—I liked to name my vehicles —and kicked the clutch. The engine roared to life. Nix and Del followed, and we peeled out of the lot, leaving the dingy yellow light of the bar behind.

Our headlights illuminated the dirt road as we sped through the night. Huge fig trees dotted the path on either side, their twisted trunks and roots forming an eerie corridor. Elephant-ear sized leaves swayed in the wind, a dark emerald that gleamed in the light.

Jungle animals howled, and enormous lightning bugs flitted along the path. They were too big to be regular bugs, so they were most likely some kind of fairy, but I wasn't going to stop to investigate. There were dangerous creatures in the jungle at night —one of the reasons we hadn't wanted to go now—and in our world, fairies could be considered dangerous.

Especially if you called them lightning bugs.

A roar sounded in the distance, echoing through the jungle and making the leaves rustle on either side as small animals scurried for safety.

The roar came again, only closer.

Then another, and another.

"Oh shit," I muttered. This was bad.

~~~

You can get a free ebook version of *Hidden Magic* by signing up for my mailing list at www.linseyhall.com/subscribe.

AUTHOR'S NOTE

Thank you so much for reading *Origin of Magic!* If you've read any of my other books, you won't be surprised to hear that I included historical elements. If you're interested in learning more about that, read on. At the end, I'll talk a bit about why Nix and her *deirfiúr* are treasure hunters and how I try to make that fit with archaeology's ethics (which don't condone treasure hunting, as I'm sure you might have guessed).

Nix's village was inspired by Saint-Guilhem-le-Désert in southwestern France, an ancient city that ascends a valley between two mountains, and by the portrayal of Themyscira in 2017's Wonder Woman movie. To my eye, Themyscira, Wonder Woman's home, looked like Saint-Guilhem-le-Désert on steroids. Both places are beautiful and trapped away from time, which made them perfect places for Nix to grow up. I did my best to describe the city of Saint-Guilhem-le-Désert, but one of the most interesting parts that was hard to fit into the book were the fountains that ran all along the street. They are fed constantly by the rivers and are always flowing, draining into a basin and then down onto the slanted cobblestone street. They are an incredibly impressive piece of ancient architecture.

Death Valley was chosen the perfect place to test Nix's skills. Where better to put *Life* than in Death Valley? Though Death Valley was given its name by a group of pioneers in 1949-50, Native Americans from the Timbisha Shoshone Tribe have lived there for over a thousand years. Many of the obstacles in the book were inspired by real places in Death Valley: Mesquite Flat Sand Dunes, Ubehebe Crater, and Badwater Basin, a dried-up ancient lake that is the lowest point in America. All sorts of minerals and metals have been mined in Death Valley over the years, including gold. Abandoned mines and towns scatter the landscape there, long since abandoned.

That's it for the historical influences in *Origin of Magic.* However, one of the most important things about this book is how Nix and her *deirfiúr* treat artifacts and their business, Ancient Magic.

As I'm sure you know, archaeology isn't quite like Indiana Jones (for which I'm both grateful and bitterly disappointed). Sure, it's exciting and full of travel. However, booby-traps are not as common as I expected. Total number of booby-traps I have encountered in my career: zero. Still hoping, though.

When I chose to write a series about archaeology and treasure hunting, I knew I had a careful line to tread. There is a big difference between these two activities. As much as I value artifacts, they are not treasure. Not even the gold artifacts. They are pieces of our history that contain valuable information, and as such, they belong to all of us. Every artifact that is excavated should be properly conserved and stored in a museum so that everyone can have access to our history. No one single person can own history, and I believe very strongly that individuals should not own artifacts. Treasure hunting is the pursuit of artifacts for personal gain.

So why did I make Nix and her *deirfiúr* treasure hunters? I'd have loved to call them archaeologists, but nothing about their work is like archaeology. Archaeology is a very laborious, painstaking process—and it certainly doesn't involve selling arti-facts. That wouldn't work for the fast-paced, adventurous series that I had planned for *Dragon's Gift*. Not to mention the fact that dragons are famous for coveting treasure. Considering where the *deirfiúr* got their skills from, it just made sense to call them trea-sure hunters.

Even though I write urban fantasy, I strive for accuracy. The *deirfiúr* don't engage in archaeological practices—therefore, I cannot call them archaeologists. I also have a duty as an archaeol-ogist to properly represent my field and our goals—namely, to protect and share history. Treasure hunting doesn't do this. One of the biggest battles that archaeology faces today is protecting cultural heritage from thieves.

I debated long and hard about not only what to call the hero-ines of this series, but also about how they would do their jobs. I wanted it to involve all the cool things we think about when we think about archaeology—namely, the Indiana Jones stuff, whether it's real or not. But I didn't know quite how to do that while still staying within the bounds of my own ethics. I can cut myself and other writers some slack because this is fiction, but I couldn't go too far into smash and grab treasure hunting.

I consulted some of my archaeology colleagues to get their take, which was immensely helpful. Wayne Lusardi, the State Maritime Archaeologist for Michigan, and Douglas Inglis and Veronica Morris, both archaeologists for Interactive Heritage, were immensely helpful with ideas. My biggest problem was figuring out how to have the heroines steal artifacts from tombs and then sell them and still sleep at night. Everything I've just said is pretty counter to this, right?

That's where the magic comes in. The heroines aren't after the artifacts themselves (they put them back where they found them, if you recall)—they're after the magic that the artifacts contain. They're more like magic hunters than treasure hunters. That solved a big part of my problem. At least they were putting the artifacts back. Though that's not proper archaeology, I could let it pass. At least it's clear that they believe they shouldn't keep the artifact or harm the site. But the SuperNerd in me said, "Well, that magic is part of the artifact's context. It's important to the artifact and shouldn't be removed and sold."

Now *that* was a problem. I couldn't escape my SuperNerd self, so I was in a real conundrum. Fortunately, that's where the immensely intelligent Wayne Lusardi came in. He suggested that the magic could have an expiration date. If the magic wasn't used before it decayed, it could cause huge problems. Think explosions and tornado spells run amok. It could ruin the entire site, not to mention possibly cause injury and death. That would be very bad.

So now you see why Nix and her *deirfiúr* don't just steal artifacts to sell them. Not only is selling the magic cooler, it's also better from an ethical standpoint, especially if the magic was going to cause problems in the long run. These aren't perfect solutions—the perfect solution would be sending in a team of archaeologists to carefully record the site and remove the dangerous magic—but that wouldn't be a very fun book.

Thanks again for reading (especially if you got this far!). I hope you enjoyed the story and will stick with Nix on the rest of her adventure!

ACKNOWLEDGMENTS

Thank you, Ben, for everything. There would be no books without you.

Thank you to Jena O'Connor and Adam at Fine Point Publishing for your excellent editing. The book is immensely better because of you both! Thank you to Crystal Jeffs, for your keen eye for continuity. Thank you to Rebecca Frank for the cover art and to Orina Kafe for the cover edits. Thanks to Stanley Morrison for his inspiring artwork--be sure to check out his amazing dragon art.

The Dragon's Gift series is a product of my two lives: one as an archaeologist and one as a novelist. Combining these two took a bit of work. I'd like to thank my friends, Wayne Lusardi, the State Maritime Archaeologist for Michigan, and Douglas Inglis and Veronica Morris, both archaeologists for Interactive Heritage, for their ideas about how to have a treasure hunter heroine that doesn't conflict too much with archaeology's ethics. The Author's Note contains a bit more about this if you are interested.

I'd also like to thank The FireSouls on Facebook for your help with ideas and clever suggestions. While I can't always use them all, it's so fun to talk about them with you. A few of those that made it into the book were Jim O'Keefe's idea for a magical signature being the scent of an 'old shoe housing a wet ferret'. Kara Perring suggested the Australian underground city of Coober Pedy as a great location for the book. I used it as inspiration for a scene in Death Valley. Charlotte Sanchez and Stacey Miller reminded me that Nix would obviously conjure something cheesy for breakfast. Alison Claxton and Jessie L. Collins suggested thermite as a hot-burning substance, and Gena Williams came up with "hairspray" (which gave birth to one of my favorite fight scenes). And Tara Patterson-Syrnyk, Kelly Ard, Guin DeLany Worthington, Tara Christensen, Michelle Gong, Sara Weir, Sally Strugnell, J Michael Gunn, Kara Perring, Kate Fox, Livvi Richardson, An Na, Janice Rosa, and Nje Dalena all suggested Dragonfruit. Please excuse me if I missed any names, and thank you all for being part of the group!

GLOSSARY

Alpha Council - There are two governments that enforce law for supernaturals—the Alpha Council and the Order of the Magica. The Alpha Council governs all shifters. They work cooperatively with the Alpha Council when necessary—for example, when capturing FireSouls.

Blood Sorceress - A type of Magica who can create magic using blood.

Conjurer - A Magica who uses magic to create something from nothing. They cannot create magic, but if there is magic around them, they can put that magic into their conjuration.

Dark Magic - The kind that is meant to harm. It's not necessarily bad, but it often is.

Deirfiúr - Sisters in Irish.

Demons - Often employed to do evil. They live in various hells but can be released upon the earth if you know how to get to them and then get them out. If they are killed on Earth, they are sent back to their hell.

Dragon Sense - A FireSoul's ability to find treasure. It is an internal sense that pulls them toward what they seek. It is easiest to find gold, but they can find anything or anyone that is valued by someone.

Elemental Mage – A rare type of mage who can manipulate all of the elements.

Enchanted Artifacts – Artifacts can be imbued with magic that lasts after the death of the person who put the magic into the artifact (unlike a spell that has not been put into an artifact—these spells disappear after the Magica's death). But magic is not stable. After a period of time—hundreds or thousands of years depending on the circumstance—the magic will degrade. Eventually, it can go bad and cause many problems.

Fire Mage – A mage who can control fire.

FireSoul - A very rare type of Magica who shares a piece of the dragon's soul. They can locate treasure and steal the gifts (powers) of other supernaturals. With practice, they can manipulate the gifts they steal, becoming the strongest of that gift. They are despised and feared. If they are caught, they are thrown in the Prison of Magical Deviants.

The Great Peace - The most powerful piece of magic ever created. It hides magic from the eyes of humans.

Hearth Witch – A Magica who is versed in magic relating to hearth and home. They are often good at potions and protective spells and are also very perceptive when on their own turf.

Informa - A supernatural who can steal powers.

Magica - Any supernatural who has the power to create magic —witches, sorcerers, mages. All are governed by the Order of the Magica.

The Origin - The descendent of the original alpha shifter. They are the most powerful shifter and can turn into any species.

Order of the Magica - There are two governments that enforce law for supernaturals—the Alpha Council and the Order of the Magica. The Order of the Magica govern all Magica. They work cooperatively with the Alpha Council when necessary—for example, when capturing FireSouls.

Phantom - A type of supernatural that is similar to a ghost. They are incorporeal. They feed off the misery and pain of others, forcing them to relive their greatest nightmares and fears. They do not have a fully functioning mind like a human or supernatural. Rather, they are a shadow of their former selves. Half-bloods are extraordinarily rare.

Seeker - A type of supernatural who can find things. FireSouls often pass off their dragon sense as Seeker power.

Shifter - A supernatural who can turn into an animal. All are governed by the Alpha Council.

Transporter - A type of supernatural who can travel anywhere. Their power is limited and must regenerate after each use.

Vampire - Blood drinking supernaturals with great strength and speed who live in a separate realm.

Warden of the Underworld - A one of a kind position created by Roarke. He keeps order in the Underworld.

ABOUT LINSEY

Before becoming a writer, Linsey Hall was a nautical archaeologist who studied shipwrecks from Hawaii and the Yukon to the UK and the Mediterranean. She credits fantasy and historical romances with her love of history and her career as an archaeologist. After a decade of tromping around the globe in search of old bits of stuff that people left lying about, she settled down and started penning her own romance novels. Her Dragon's Gift series draws upon her love of history and the paranormal elements that she can't help but include.

COPYRIGHT

35388118R00125